ONE MORE NIGHT

J. AKRIDGE

Cover Design: Kari March Designs

Editing: EAL Editing Services

Formatting: J. Akridge

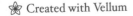 Created with Vellum

This one is for everyone who fell in love with Kyle and Tessa in One Night, then begged to learn more about Lou's story.

Lou was never meant to have a story, but the more readers began to ask, a story began to form. I sat down one day, and I remember it all very vividly. I do not plot my books, it's a struggle for me, but with Lou's story I was able to write out every single chapter and every detail that would take place.

I think that means it was meant to be.

I hope you love their story as much as I do.

PROLOGUE

Fifteen Years Earlier

"Why are you doing this? What did I do wrong?" I ask, the tears burning the back of my eyelids. I feel my heart shattering in my chest, and I hate it. I don't know how to fix it, or how to get him to listen to me.

It wasn't supposed to be this way. We were supposed to get married, have children, and live a long life together. It's what we always planned.

Why is he doing this? To me? To us? To our future?

Declan is my best friend and my soulmate. I know I won't ever get over this type of heartache if he walks away.

He turns, walking away from me. I reach out, grabbing his elbow and spin him to face me. His brown hair falls to his forehead as he settles, he looks everywhere but at me.

"Talk to me," I demand. "It's the least you could do." For a moment, I see his wall start to collapse. His eyes soften as he looks at me, I just need to understand why he's doing this to us. "Is this about your dad?" And just like that, that simple question causes that wall to slide back into place. A stone mask covering his face now, not letting me in. "Just talk to me, we can work this out. Please!" I beg.

"It has to be this way, Lou." His green eyes bounce between mine. The look he gives me exposes my biggest fear. He's leaving, he's done, and there's nothing I can do or say right now that's going to change that. "Go home," he mutters before he turns and walks away again.

This time I don't stop him, I watch as he disappears. My feet are rooted to the ground beneath me, and I'm unable to move. So many emotions are flooding me right now, but at the same time... I feel numb.

He reaches his truck, hand frozen on the handle as his head falls forward against the window before he climbs into it. I watch and wait, knowing he's going to climb out and come back to me. He'll tell me it's all a mistake and that he's just struggling with the death of his father. It's only been two weeks, that's normal to still feel emotions like this, right? I've never lost anyone in my life, so I'm not sure what that feels like.

Maybe I wasn't there enough for him. If he needed some time to himself, I could have given him that. I would do anything for him, doesn't he know that?

His head never turns in my direction as he backs out of his parking spot and drives in the opposite direction of his house. We live in a small town, where everyone knows everyone and there's only one place that road leads... and it's far away from here.

Realization sets in that he isn't coming back. He broke up with me. He left me here and broke my heart.

I collapse to the ground beneath me, feeling the weight

of my broken relationship on top of me. I don't fight the tears as they fall, my entire world just drove away without an explanation.

I'll never get over Declan Sanchez.

Ever.

1

LOU

SOME DAYS I still ask myself how I got in this position.

The one where I'm tired of coming home, even after twelve and fourteen hour days, I dread being in my own home. Being at work is still better than coming home any day. Especially when the home is somewhere I don't feel wanted.

Which is ridiculous, because I bought it. The entire damn thing belongs to me, but yet every day when my shift ends, I'd rather sleep in my car in the parking lot of the clinic.

Peter and I aren't happy, we haven't been for a while but I haven't figured out the best way to end things. I think part of it is being in my mid-thirties and feeling like a failure if I'm not on track to get married soon. All of my friends are married, have kids, and the perfect little home. I'm envious of them, which is pathetic on my part.

Hell, even my brother has a picture perfect life. Even if it wasn't planned.

I smile to myself, thinking of the love they have for eachother.

When Tessa, my brother's new wife, walked into my office, I never knew what the future was going to hold and I had no clue that she was pregnant by my brother at the time. I took to her immediately, and did everything I could even before knowing she was carrying my brother's child, to help her. She was alone here, the only people she knew were the ones at the real estate company.

I've watched my brother turn into a man, right before my eyes. He was a bachelor, the one that slept with a different girl nearly every night. It's why he kept the little apartment above his bar instead of renting it out.

Sometimes, I'm even jealous of them. When I look at my niece and nephew, I want that life.

All I want is love, true love.

But I think someone only experiences that type of love once in their life, and unfortunately for me, that time has passed.

Declan was supposed to be my one, and I feel it deep in my soul. I didn't start dating again after him until I was opening my own practice. My heart wasn't in it, and I emotionally had nothing to give.

When Declan drove away from me, fifteen years ago, I was dead inside. It's probably the only reason I pushed through to become an OBGYN. The plan was always to go to nursing school, and that was it. After he left, I had nothing else in my life for me, so I pushed my ass as hard as I could every day and studied, making sure I had straight A's.

It worked, because here I am today. I graduated early with honors and I'm walking into *my* practice, where I continue to pour my heart every single day. Granted, I got lucky when Dr. Millings was retiring and let me buy the practice from him, but either way, after working under that man and kicking ass every day in school, I deserve it.

"Goodmorning," my receptionist, Talia, greets me as I walk through. "It's getting colder." She smiles.

Talia hasn't been with me long, but I swear she's the glue to this place at this point. I'm not sure I'd know what to do without her at this point, she keeps me and everyone else in line and keeps this place flowing smoothly.

"Morning, Talia." I smile back at her. "It really is." I shiver at the thought. I'm not the biggest fan of winter, but I do enjoy fall.

After the stunt my last receptionist pulled with my sister-in-law when she was pregnant, I knew it was time to cut my ties. We had known each other a long time, which is probably the only reason I left her on my staff as long as I did.

Everyone complained about her, in one way or another. My brother couldn't stand her, but he'd sit his pretty ass at the front desk and make her think she had a chance with him each time he came in.

Just the thought of him flirting with her makes me want to throw up.

I even invited her to their baby shower, which was the dumbest thing I've possibly ever done. And I've done a lot of stupid shit over the years. But apparently, I was blinded by our friendship to see the true side of Vivian.

Either way, I have Talia now and she's amazing. I

couldn't ask for a better person to run my clinic. Everything is organized and the clients adore her. My daily complaints about staff went to nearly zero once Vivian was out the door.

I check on the schedule for the day before heading to my office to get ready for my first patient. I wave at a few of the nurses as I pass, they're already booting up their iPads and getting ready for the day.

I unlock my door, pushing it open before I step inside. I shut the door behind me and sit in my chair. Just need a moment, that's all I need. My head's swimming with the fight Peter and I had this morning. It's *always* something, and it's draining me in more ways than one. He's been so secretive lately, it makes me feel like he's unfaithful but I don't have any proof of it.

My phone vibrates in my hand, Tessa's name flashes across the screen when I look down.

Lifting it, I slide my thumb across the bottom before answering. "Hello."

"Hey, you." She pauses, saying something to the twins. They're already two years old and I don't know where the time went. "What are you doing after work tonight?"

"Uh..." I think about my plans and realize I have nothing to do because Peter is either never home or doesn't speak when I am. "Nothing." I shrug my shoulders.

"Let's have a night out. Kyle offered to stay home tonight since it's a Wednesday and not as busy as the weekends." She laughs. "He just hired a new bartender and I think this is his way of having us scope the kid out while he's working."

"I'm game, want me to invite Nicole?"

"Already did. Chloe is coming, too. We will pick you up

at seven, be ready." She laughs before hanging up the phone.

————

I'VE BEEN SITTING HERE for thirty minutes, staring at the clock above my desk slowly tick with the passing time. When it finally strikes six, I stand and grab my things before turning the light off and locking the door behind me. When I walk up front, I'm expecting to be alone but Talia is still here.

"What are you still doing here?" I ask, dropping my bag to her desk. I look over at the clock on her desk just to make sure it matches the one in my office, and it does.

"I was finishing up some billing, and wanted to get ahead before Friday rolls around." She smiles, clicking a few buttons on her keyboard before pushing her chair back. "I feel like I spend most of my day rushing to get billing entered before I leave." She laughs. "And we all know the weekends aren't long enough."

"They're not," I lie. If it were up to me and I could do everything here on my own, I'd be open on the weekends too if it kept me from going home.

I think of Talia, wondering if her catching up on billing is really what's keeping her here later or if she's avoiding going home like I am.

I glance at the door then back to Talia. "Hey, what are you doing tonight?"

"Nothing." She smirks. "Literally nothing. I have no life outside of work, I've been living with my parents since I moved back home. No boyfriend, I'm boring." She laughs, shrugging her shoulders.

Talia is closer to Tessa's age, and takes classes at the local community college when she isn't at work. I don't know how she does it all.

"Wanna have a girls night?" I ask. "I can introduce you to some friends of mine and my sister-in-law."

Her eyes light up and she's nodding before I even finish the sentence.

I reach over the desk, grabbing a notepad and pen to write my address down on. "Here's my address." I scribble on it. "We're leaving at seven."

Handing it to her, she follows me out the door and we separate at our cars.

"See you in a little bit." Talia smiles before climbing into her car with a small wave.

The drive to my house is short, it was one of the appealing things when I bought it because it was a short commute to work. Pulling into my driveway, I hit the button to open my garage doors before pulling inside.

Peter's truck isn't here, and it's odd that it gives me relief and worry at the same time. I'm relieved he isn't home, because I don't have to deal with explaining where I'll be for the rest of the night. When I'm working, he complains about it and when I'm home he doesn't act like I exist.

Shutting my car off, I grab my phone to text him and let him know my plans for the night. Even though we're struggling right now, I at least want to let him know where I'll be. You know, thoughtful girlfriend and all.

ME: Hey. Just got home from work. I'm heading out with Tessa and the girls for a bit. See you when I get home?

Peter: Yeah

That's his only response. Just one word.

It's times like this where my mind starts to wonder who I was fifteen years ago.

How can feelings for someone that completely shattered your heart still be so strong?

2

DECLAN

"Mr. Sanchez." Dr. Tinnin waves his hand in front of my face.

I shake my head and run my hand over my face, trying to wash away the memories that Dr. Tinnin always brings up when I'm here.

"What are you thinking about right now?"

"I don't want to talk about it," I tell him, honestly.

It's the *last* thing I want to talk about. I never want to talk about it.

Our orders came in this morning, we were ready not long after that. A woman and her child are being held captive by a sadistic asshole. The only thing she's done wrong is being American and on Arabic soil. She chose the wrong place to go for her mission trip with her church. And to make matters worse, she brought her pre-teen daughter along with her.

Now both are being held captive, and from what we can see they're shackled to a wall near the center of the building.

"Fuck," I murmur to myself. I've got to figure out a plan to get my men inside, we're running out of time.

I look over at one of my men, Nick Benson. He's my second, and damn good at his job. It's why he's in our unit. Separate, we're all badass, sure... But together, we're lethal.

"This is what we're going to do." I rattle off directions, he nods his heavy head before relaying everything I've just said to Will behind him.

Slowly, my men start moving to surround the house. I hold a hand up to halt all movement, once we've reached along the side of the house. We're hidden in the night sky, but we can never be too careful so I hold our positions and wait for any sign that they've caught on to our movement. Gunnar stands at attention, tucked closely against my leg.

Once I'm sure we're in the clear, I take a deep breath and point two fingers for Benson to round me. He does, Will coming up behind him with a breaching device in his hands.

"Go," I say, only loud enough for my men to hear.

Will slams the breacher into the wooden door, it flies open with a thud, nearly shattering as it hits the wall behind it. Benson tosses in a stun grenade as we all turn our backs to protect ourselves from the sound.

People on the inside begin screaming, and I realize there are other women and children inside, but they aren't American. They're screaming in what sounds like Arabic and it makes my stomach turn to know that they live here, knowing these men are keeping innocent people hostage.

The dogs are sent in first, we each file through, guns raised and pointed around the room. Gunshots begin ringing out around us, I fire two shots. One hitting a man directly in the chest while the other is hit between the eyes. Gunnar disappears into the smoky room, and I have to remind myself that he's working and knows his job.

I move to a hallway, following behind him but drop to my

knees to peer around the edge. I search for any sight of Gunnar when Benson taps on my shoulder, letting me know he's there for backup. I move slowly, using all the training we've had and keeping my adrenaline in check.

I'm looking for one thing, and one thing only. The woman and her daughter.

We clear two rooms, but come up empty. Moving to the third, the door opens just as I start to grab the knob. A gun is pointed directly at my face, brushing against my temple.

The man in front of me doesn't look to my side, so he doesn't see Benson next to me. My eyes scan the room behind him, and I'm met with the eyes of the woman we've been called here for. The color of her blue eyes remind me of a set I used to stare into at home. Her light blonde hair is nearly the exact same shade, and if I hadn't spent hours earlier studying the looks of this woman, I'd swear they were a damn match.

She has bruising along her jaw, one eye is swollen shut, her clothing has been ripped, and blood is caked in her hair.

Her daughter is tied up in the corner, her pants are gone but she isn't in nearly as bad of shape as her mother. At least not physically that is. A dingy white piece of fabric is wrapped around her eyes, which is probably a good thing considering the state of her mother's looks right now.

"Ah. The American soldiers," the man says, spitting in my direction. He leaves his gun pressed against my forehead. "You were almost too late for the show."

I don't respond, not giving him the satisfaction he's wanting by answering him right now.

"Your American women, they're feisty."

The fury builds inside of me, hearing him talk about them in this way. I don't know either one of these women, but I doubt they deserved anything like this in their lifetimes.

"That one was a virgin." His accent so thick, I almost can't understand him, but he confirms to me that he's raped her and that makes me feel like the biggest piece of shit because I didn't get here sooner to save her from that.

She's barely a teenager, and now she'll have years and years of therapy to try to cope with the things she and her mother have been through here. It'll threaten her faith, and that's what pisses me off about people like this...

I grunt, unable to control it and his eyes snap to mine. He pulls the gun away from my forehead, pointing it at the mother and pulls the trigger. I watch in slow motion as her lifeless body topples to the ground, but the only thing I see is Lou.

It's not this mother on a mission trip with her daughter, it's Lou that floats through my mind.

Raising my gun, I fire shot after shot into the man. Not letting up until Nick steps in behind me, grabbing my shoulder to stop me. He releases me and moves to where the daughter is, slowly untying her and identifying himself as American while he does it.

We saved her.

But not before we lost her mother, probably the most important person in the world to her.

I stand, staring at the woman laying on the ground and struggle to find my breath.

"Declan." Dr. Tinnin snaps his fingers. "Where'd you go?"

"It was her," I say, trying to catch my breath. The tears burn at the back of my eyes, but I never let them fall.

"Yes, you thought the woman was Lou, your ex-girlfriend," he says slowly, watching my reaction to his words.

I stand, pushing the seat back. "Alright, I can't do anymore today," I tell him. "Umm, when am I going to be cleared for duty?"

"Declan, I think we should talk about that." He pulls his thin framed glasses from his eyes, setting them down on the arm of his chair. "I've been in contact with your Commander, you will be placed on mandatory leave for the time being."

"What?"

"I think it's crucial, if you want to continue your career, to confront the issues you've been experiencing." He holds a hand up when he senses I'm going to interrupt him, so I bite back my words and let him finish. "I know you've been through a lot, and watching that woman die was not easy for you, especially when she looks like someone you care very much about... but I don't think your issues are just with that situation. I think it goes deeper than that." He writes something down on his notepad. "I think you should go home, take some time to reflect on your life before the military."

I don't listen to anymore of what he has to say, instead I turn to leave, swinging the door open and making sure it's heard through his office as I walk out.

He may have a doctorate in psychology, but he doesn't fucking know me.

3

LOU

"READY, BITCH?" Nicole shouts from the passenger seat of Tessa's SUV. "Or bitches?" she says when she sees Talia following behind me.

"Hey, this is Talia." I gesture to her before opening the back door of the SUV. "She is the receptionist that replaced Vivian."

"Good riddance," they both say in unison, making all of us laugh.

"Was she really that bad?" Talia asks, sliding in behind me and shutting the door.

Tessa and Nicole both turn around to look at us from the front seat.

"She was horrible." Tessa points out.

I look over at Talia as she's buckling her seat belt. "See, I wasn't lying."

"No, you weren't." She laughs. "So, how do you all know each other?" Talia asks, looking around at the three of us.

"Well, Lou and I went to high school together," Nicole says smirking. "A long ass time ago."

"Hey!" I shout. "I'm not that old, *yet.*"

"Honey, we're nearing our mid-thirties. It's downhill from here, babe," she jokes.

Talia looks at Tessa.

"*And,*" Tessa chimes in, turning her attention back to the front of the vehicle. She shifts it into drive, checks her mirror and then pulls away from the curb. "I had a one night stand with Lou's brother and ended up pregnant by him, only to run into him in Lou's office."

The car is silent as we look at Talia's face, trying to decipher what's running through her head right now.

"I don't know what you want me to say to that," Talia says calmly.

We all burst into laughter. The look on Talia's face only makes me laugh harder, I lean forward but the seatbelt jerks me back into place. Tessa swerves, laughing so hard that Nicole has to grab ahold of the wheel.

"Holy hell, don't kill us all. It took me forever to get my hair curled with the spawns of satan running around tonight," Nicole shouts. "Damn."

Nicole has three children with her husband, Roger. All boys, and she is seriously one of the most perfect boy moms I've ever seen. Her oldest just turned six, then she has a four year old and the last baby was a surprise and he just turned three.

"Stop it," I tell her. "They are sweet little angel babies."

"The hell they are," she mutters, turning in her seat so that she's facing me. "Cooper dumped my wax warmer on the living room carpet before I left."

Cooper is her three year old, and he is taking the terrible three's thing extremely seriously.

"Okay, maybe he is a spawn," Tessa adds. "Did you get it out of your carpet? I'd be pissed."

"I left it for Roger to clean up." She chuckles. "They're his spawns tonight. It's Momma's night off."

A few minutes later, we pull up outside of my brother's bar, parking in his designated spot along the back wall. Perks of being the wife I guess, because being the sister doesn't get me shit except a discount once a month.

"Kyle said to enter through the front door so that the new guy doesn't know who we are." She points in the direction for us to go. We all fall into step beside one another, Tessa links her arm with mine.

"He's really being like that tonight?" I joke.

"Oh, yeah." She giggles. "It's been so long since he's hired anyone like this so he's going overboard. Anytime I point it out to him, he gets all pissy."

"He's too much," Nicole tells her.

"He really is." Tessa laughs as we step around the corner to the front of the building, my brother's sign hangs above the door.

Arrow.

I follow them all inside, letting the door shut behind me. A few customers glance our way from the sound, but most just turn back to whatever they were doing before we came in.

The twinkling lights hanging from the ceiling catch my attention like always, but this time they're slightly different. They're not the normal white color that hangs, instead they're a light amber color. It makes the room darker, but not so dark that it's difficult to see.

The door is angled, so as soon as we step in, we can see the entire bar from where we're standing. The large pieces of tin metal are hung on the back walls, giving it the popular rustic vibe that everyone strives for now. My brother's really worked hard on this place, and I honestly don't give him enough credit for all that he's done.

He has neon lights hanging on every wall advertising the different types of alcohol he serves. The wooden bar top stretches from one end to the other, with large, leather wrapped stools that are evenly placed along it. Several high tables are scattered around in different areas, which was my idea. Don't mind me while I pat myself on the back.

I prefer high tables if I can snatch one, don't ask me why... I just do.

An entire row of booths are lined along the back of the open room, with large televisions hanging from the walls. All hosting the newest sporting event.

It's pretty quiet in here tonight, not as loud as it is on the weekends, but between the people talking and the music playing it has a nice hum. We take one of the open high tables, each of us hanging our purses from the back of our chairs. I look over at Tony who's working on mixing a few drinks for two girls.

Tony's been with my brother for as long as I can remember. I'm not even sure how their friendship started, if you want to call it that. It's more professional, but the two of them get along so well that it makes this place run smoothly. Kyle knows he'd be lost without Tony behind the bar.

I watch as the two girls hang on his every word, like most who come in here do. Since my brother is no longer a single man, all the girls tend to flock to Tony and he loves the attention from them. I don't think he'll ever get married, he enjoys his bachelor lifestyle far too much.

But then again, I said that about my brother too and look at him now. He's married with twins and is the happiest I have ever seen him.

"What do you want to drink?" Tessa asks us all as she leans against the table to hear what we want. "Oh, there's Chloe."

"Hey, sorry I'm late. I had a late showing and couldn't get out of there." Chloe walks over to our table and drops her purse in an open chair.

"That's okay," Tessa tells her, she looks to Talia to introduce the two of them. "Talia, this is my best friend, Chloe. Chloe, this is Talia. She works for Lou, replaced that whore."

Chloe snorts. "About damn time."

"I know, I know." I wave her off. "She's gone though, and the clinic is better off now."

"Damn right it is." Chloe chuckles. "I'm going to use the restroom, get me a beer?"

Tessa nods. "What do you all want?"

Talia and Nicole both tell her what they want before she turns to me. "I'll go with you," I say, standing from my seat.

I follow behind her as she heads toward the bar, finding an empty spot right in the new guy's section. Tony looks in our direction before giving Tessa a wink.

The new guy approaches, tossing a rag over his shoulder. "What can I get you beautiful ladies tonight?"

"I need two Sex on the Beaches, a Michelob Ultra, a strawberry margarita, and..." she trails off, looking at me.

"Whatever you have on tap is fine."

He nods, turning to fix our drinks.

"So far, so good," she whispers so he can't hear us. He

slides my beer in front of me, and gets started on her margarita. "Are you new here? Uh, I don't know your name." She laughs. "I don't think I've seen you before."

"Yeah, Marshall." He reaches across the bar and shakes her hand. "I just started. Tonight's my first night on my own." He smiles at her.

"Ah. That makes sense then." Tessa looks over at me, the corner of her mouth lifting in a smirk and I know she's now taking this task from Kyle a little more serious. "Like it so far? I heard the boss is a dick."

I nearly choke on my beer when she says it. I wasn't expecting it. Tessa never talks like this, at least not to people she doesn't know. But now I'm intrigued because I have got to hear what the fate of this newbie's current job is.

"Ah, Kyle?"

Tessa nods.

"He's great. I've learned a lot from him."

"Oh."

I can't hold it in, my laugh bubbles out of me and I nearly fall off my bar stool and spill part of my beer in the process. Tessa looks like something just kicked her damn puppy. She was obviously expecting a different answer from the kid.

"But, I hear his wife is really nice." Marshall looks at Tessa and winks.

I snort. I fucking snort, so loud that the people sitting in Tony's section of the bar look our way, earning me an amused smirk from Tony.

"You knew who I was?" she asks.

"Yeah," he laughs now, "I saw your picture on his desk during my interview."

"Oh, my God." She slaps her forehead with the palm of her hand. "I'm sorry."

He shakes his head, waving her off. "Not a big deal, I'd expect nothing less from him." He sits a few of our drinks on a tray for us to carry to the table. "Report back to him that everything is going good."

"I will."

He turns to finish up the rest of our order.

"So, how are the kids?" I turn to Tessa and ask while we wait.

"They're good. Lucy was mad that I was seeing you tonight and she wasn't."

"I'll come get them tomorrow and take them to the park." My niece and nephew are the best, some of the greatest damn kids I've ever met and I've delivered a ton of them. They're mature for their ages, I mean as mature as one can be at two, but they don't really throw a lot of tantrums, and they're so smart. They really are the best version of their parents.

"They'll love that," she tells me.

"Here you go." Marshall slides the other three drinks in front of us with a smile.

"Thanks," Tessa says. "You can just put it on a tab, my husband will pay it tomorrow." She laughs.

"Bro," Tony says, tossing an arm over his shoulder. "Did you pass?"

"You knew?" he mutters.

Tessa holds her hand up for Tony to high five. He smacks his against hers without hesitation, slowly smiling.

"Asshole." Marshall laughs, shaking his head in amusement.

"He did." Tessa smiles at him as we hop down from the bar and head back to our table.

After we've gotten a few more drinks in our systems, we're all laughing and having a good time. I can't even describe how much this night out with the girls was needed. It's been so long since I've done this, that it's really showing me how miserable I am with my own life. It's not heading in the direction I ever thought it would, and right now I just really feel *stuck*.

Talia tells us about her ex boyfriend, and how she thinks he resembles *Mr. Bean* now. I can't get the image out of my head, Talia and Mr. Bean.

"My God, how horrible was that when you had sex?" Chloe asks.

Nicole barks out a laugh that causes us all to join in.

"Honestly, he was a damn freak in the sheets." Talia looks over at me, blushing slightly.

"Girl, we're friends tonight. I'm not your boss." I laugh, clinking my near empty glass with hers.

"Ohhhh... do tell," Chloe urges. "I'm not really getting any these days, so I need to live through you."

"What happened to the guy you were seeing?" Tessa tilts her head in question.

"He turned out to be just like the others..." Chloe shrugs. "He didn't understand that when I agreed to date him, I had this expectation of him only dating me."

"Asshole," Tessa mutters, throwing an arm over her shoulder. "It's okay, I'll be your boyfriend."

"Damn right." Chloe laughs, pressing a kiss to Tessa's cheek.

The only way I know how to describe their relationship is to compare them to Merideth and Christina on Grey's

Anatomy. If you replace the surgeon career with being real estate agents, you've got the two of them. I'm surprised Kyle hasn't woken up with Chloe in bed with them yet. For all I know, he has and just hasn't told me about it.

The conversation gets quiet for a moment after that, we dance next to the table and just vibe to the song playing. When it changes to a slower tune, one of Adele's newest songs, *Easy On Me,* my mind bounces back to Peter. The lyrics in the song resonate with me, reminding me how I have never gotten a chance to feel the world around me.

I've either been with Declan, burying myself in school, or trying to make things work with Peter. I feel like I've always put him first in our relationship, and somehow I forgot to take care of myself.

But now I give up.

In this moment, I feel it deep in my bones what my next step will be. I need to put myself first for once, and do things that will make me happy. Regardless of how difficult they'll be, I have to start living again. Living for myself.

"I think I'm going to leave Peter," I blurt out, suddenly covering my mouth as every set of eyes at the table slowly turn in my direction. I didn't mean to say it, at least not outloud. I don't know if I needed to hear the words for myself, or if I needed all of my friends to hear it.

"What?" Tessa leans forward a little on her seat. She searches my face, looking for any hint that I'm joking, but I'm not.

This is what I have to do. They'll understand, right?

"I think it's time." I take a drink, trying to disguise the fact that I'm nearly shaking from my announcement. It's not that I'm regretting the words, or my decision... but this is big. It's a life changing moment for me. "I'm miserable." My voice breaks, and the emotions start to flood me.

"Oh, Lou." Her shoulders drop, feeling sorry for me. She moves closer toward me.

"It's fine." I wave her off, not wanting to ruin the night we're having. But I can't deny the weight that seems to have been lifted from my shoulders. "Honestly, it'll take some adjusting to get used to being alone all the time, but it's what's best."

"What happened?" Nicole looks over to Tony, gesturing for another round of shots when he takes notice of her.

"I think he's cheating on me." A few of them gasp in surprise. "We went through this a few years ago, and I thought things had gotten better but then they went right back to where they were." I shrug, hiding the ache that hits my chest. "Things were good, but I was naive for ever thinking things would work after that. He's not interested in getting married, he never has been but I just hoped that that would change over time," I explain. "He doesn't really want kids, hell, even when Lane and Lucy come over, he barely acknowledges them."

"I didn't know things had gotten bad between y'all again." Nicole reaches over, grabbing my hand. Tony brings our drinks over, sitting them down in the middle of our table. He must realize the topic of conversation is heavy because I swear he drops the tray so damn fast you can see dust kicking up behind him on the way back to the bar.

"I just think it's time. I'm not getting any younger, and I don't really prefer to live my life alone, but it's got to be better than this shit. Plus, I'm nearly in my mid-thirties... and I'd like to have kids before I need a damn walker to keep up with them." They giggle. "I don't know why we're still doing this if we're this unhappy." I shrug, lifting my shot glass as they do the same. "I spend longer hours at work just to avoid going home."

"Is that why you're working until six or later almost every night?" Talia asks.

I nod in response.

"Well," Tessa lifts her glass up, "to new beginnings."

"And badass boss babes," Nicole chimes in.

"And to unlimited drinks because our girl is fucking the owner." Chloe holds her glass up.

We all laugh.

"And..." Talia trails off. "I got nothing to top that last one."

We all laugh again, clinking our glasses before bringing the shots to our lips.

The liquid burns going down, but numbs some of the pain I'm feeling right now. "Let's dance," I shout when one of Shania Twain's songs blares through the speakers. I swear, that woman can make me kick a fucking door down in heels when she comes on the radio.

———

TONY OFFERS to drive us all home, since none of us are the legal driving limit currently. My brother really doesn't pay him enough for this shit, I doubt when he signed on he thought he'd be driving his boss' sister, wife, and friends home from a drunken girl's night out.

Just on the short drive to everyone's houses, we've laughed, we've cried, we've fallen out of the car and had to be shoved back in because one of us thought running down the middle of the street was a good idea.

It was me, I thought it was a good idea to run down the street.

By the way, it's not. Cars don't really slow down... rude, I know.

I'm the last stop, when he pulls to the front of my house I look out the window at the perfectly trimmed lawn and the cute fall wreath that hangs on the black wooden door. No one would know the heartache that's taking place on the inside of those walls.

"Here we are." He shifts into park and looks over at me, but I try to avoid his stare. My walls are slipping now that the alcohol is wearing off slightly, and I can't let anyone see how truly broken I am right now.

"Thanks for giving me a ride," I tell him, pushing open the car door.

"Anytime, Lou." He smiles at me, and it's that smile that he gives the ladies at the bar. "I'll wait until you get inside. Goodnight."

"Night." I shove the door shut and head up the driveway to the garage door.

I type in the code and wait as it slowly rises. I give Tony a slight wave before stepping inside and hitting the transmitter before stepping inside the house.

Peter isn't home, and I'm not sure why I thought he would be. It's quiet, the sound I actually dread and one of the reasons I've probably pushed this off for as long as I have.

Being alone isn't enjoyable to me. My mind starts reeling and then I start over reacting that someone's in the house and about to get me. Even though my security system is fully armed, and I've barricaded myself into whatever room I'm having the panic attack in.

Dropping my purse to the countertop of the island, I pull my phone out and send Peter a quick text.

Me: *Tomorrow, we need to talk.*

He texts back almost immediately, as if he'd been waiting for this moment.

Peter: *Yeah, I think we do.*

I let out a sigh but don't bother responding, instead I head up the stairs and get ready for bed. My fucked up life will still be here when I wake up in the morning, the only difference is the confidence from the alcohol I've consumed tonight will have worn off and been replaced with a different kind of misery.

4

DECLAN

IT'S BEEN ten years since I've been home.

Ten years. That's a long ass time, to be away from the place you were born and raised your entire life.

I left fifteen years ago, driving away from the one and only person I've ever fully given my heart to. When I left for the Marines, I barely said goodbye to my momma. I couldn't say goodbye to Lou, either.

I did the only thing that made sense in my head, and that was to break up with her no matter how much I didn't want to do it. I couldn't handle the thought of her being upset while I was gone, and I sure as hell didn't plan on coming back. Not for her, not for my mom, not for anyone.

That was selfish, but I wasn't functioning. Not in the way I should have been then. My dad had just died, I was spiraling out of control and didn't know which way was up and which way was down.

The last time I came home, I saw Lou. She didn't see me, I made sure of that and hid behind the end cap of crackers at the local grocery store but I saw her. She still looked as gorgeous as she did in high school, even better actually. I watched her for what seemed like forever, like a fucking stalker while she chose what snacks to put in her basket.

But then I saw him. He was an alright looking dude, but nowhere near the same league as Lou. She could do so much better, but then she could also do so much better than me too.

She smiled, and normally I'd be hit with longing at the sight of it, but it was directed at him. It was the same way she used to smile at me. That was a fucking punch in the gut, to see my girl with some other dude.

I'm not dumb, I knew she'd move on eventually. I didn't expect her to wait on me to return, because she'd be waiting forever if she had. What I didn't expect was for me to see her with someone new and how I would feel about it when it happened.

Pulling into my mom's driveway, I shift my truck in park. Looking at the house I grew up in, I take a deep breath trying to fight all the sensations flowing through my body right now. My dad's been gone just over fifteen years, and the house hasn't had the normal care it had when he was here.

One of the gutters is hanging, and some of the siding has started to chip away. The gravel drive has grass covering most of it, and the mailbox looks like a good windstorm could take it out with ease.

A wave of guilt barrels into me, because I've left my mom to deal with this part of life on her own. I could have come home after my last tour, but I didn't. I stayed away because I knew that Lou had built a life here, and I was fucking terrified to see it. So scared that I tucked my tail and never returned to help take care of shit here and always had my mom come to me for visits.

A whimper from the backseat shakes me from my thoughts, I reach behind me and scratch the side of Gunnar's neck. My German Shepard has become my best friend, he served with me in the military but after an injury he received during a raid, they retired him. He barks in the direction of the house, his ears perking up in excitement and when I turn my head back in that direction I see my mom standing on the front porch.

She's aged since the last time I've seen her in person, which has been about three years. I was gone for nearly a year of that time, and the other I was working on base. Doing everything I could to avoid having to come home.

I shake my head, I'm such an asshole for making her deal with all this shit on her own. All because I couldn't be a man and accept my own fucking fate.

Pushing the door open, I climb out of the truck step-ping back enough to let Gunnar jump out behind me. His paws kick up dirt as he rushes in the direction of my mom, forgetting about me completely. I grab my bag from the back, slinging it up on my shoulder before walking in her direction.

"There's my boy." Mom smiles at me when I get halfway across the yard. Gunnar has already greeted her and is standing at attention next to her feet. At least if I decide to reenlist when my time is up, I'll feel better knowing that Gunnar is here taking care of her for me. She at least won't be lonely with him here.

Fortunately, I still have plenty of time left to make my

decision on that, which is why I'm here... trying to get my head straight so I can make up my mind.

Per the doctor's orders.

Then again, that all comes back to deciding where I'll be living. If I come home, I'll risk running into Lou every damn day for the rest of my life.

And I'm man enough to admit that I don't think I can fucking do that. Seeing her everyday, with another man... I just can't. Those feelings never died, even after all this time, they're still there and still gut me every day.

"Hi, Mama." I bend, wrapping her in my arms and squeeze. "I've missed you."

"I've missed you." She squeezes tighter before letting go and stepping toward the house. "Come inside, it's getting cooler out."

"Yeah, Fall is here isn't it?" I look back out at the yard, letting my eyes fall on the amount of leaves that are covering the dying grass. It's something I can work on for her while I'm here, along with the rest of the things I noted when I pulled in.

When I step inside behind her, I'm hit with that familiar scent. The scent that only your parents have, and it never changes. The walls are still the same tan color they were when I was in high school. The furniture hasn't been updated. The only thing that is different is the large dog bed in the corner of the living room that she's added for Gunnar.

"So." She steps into the kitchen, gesturing for the table. She pulls ice cream from the freezer and spoons some into a bowl before placing it in front of me. Butter Pecan, it was my favorite sweet dessert when I was younger, and I still eat it now. "Have you made your decision yet?"

"Mom." I blow out a breath and look at her. "I don't know what I'm going to do." I knew she'd bring it up, it's probably been bothering her since I pulled in the driveway. If it had been up to her, I never would have been able to enlist in the first place.

"Okay, okay." She holds her hands up in front of her in surrender. "I was just asking. You know what I'd like for you to do."

And I do.

I take a bite of my ice cream, trying to focus on the taste of the ice cream and not getting frustrated at her for being a mom. I'm sure most moms feel the exact same way that mine does. Looking over at Gunnar, he rests his head on my mom's lap.

"Have you been going to therapy?" she asks, normally that question would floor me, but I guess Dr. Tinnin's been helping more than I realize.

"Yeah, every week," I explain. "It's been helping since...." I trail off, thinking of the last rescue we did. How fucked up it was when all I saw was Lou being attacked, even though it wasn't Lou at all. I was too fucking late and couldn't say Maurene.

That was the woman's name.

She was there with her church, just trying to help in any way that she possibly could. I doubt she knew the type of danger she'd be put in when she signed up for it, and her daughter... fuck. That poor girl.

Abigail didn't even speak a word to us when we rescued her. Granted, I was so traumatized by thinking I saw Lou being shot by that piece of shit that I didn't even think about Abigail until we were out of the building and assessing her for any injuries.

Her mom took the most of the beating, but Abigail was raped repeatedly and tortured in her own way.

"What are you going to do while you are here?" She strokes the top of Gunnar's head, and I watch as he tilts his head to her, showing his appreciation for the affection.

"They're letting me do it virtually." Thank God. I don't think I could handle transferring to another therapist, it wasn't easy to get comfortable with the one I have now.

Not to mention how everyone would know all my fucking problems by the end of the session if I were doing it here, confidentiality or not.

"That's good." She smiles. "I didn't know that was an option."

"It's usually not, but with everything that's been going on they're allowing it," I tell her.

"Ah." She smiles. We sit in an awkward silence for a while before she speaks again. "Well, I guess I'm going to head to bed shortly. Do you need help with your things?"

"No, Mama. I got it, get some rest." I watch as she stands, struggling to get to her full height. She bends slightly, pressing a kiss to my temple before scratching behind Gunnar's ear and heading down the hallway.

"Go, boy," I tell him and he follows behind her.

She can have him tonight. I need to be alone, my emotions are threatening to overpower me and I need a quick session with my therapist before I call it a night.

The problem is that I already know what the root of my emotional issues are, I'm just too fucking stubborn to address them.

5

LOU

"Aunt Wou," Lane squeals as he goes higher on the swing. "Me higher." I smile at the use of my name, it may not be correct but I absolutely love it.

"If I push you any higher than you already are, you'll fly right off." I laugh, giving him a slight shove.

"Me, me," Lucy whines from the swing next to him, so I do the same for her.

"Wook, wook, wook." Lane starts attempting to climb to his feet to head in the direction he wants me to look, so I grab his swing and quickly stop him before lifting him out. As soon as his feet hit the ground, he's running across the pebbled ground. The gravel slows him down but he keeps pushing in that direction. Lucy starts squirming too, but instead of trying to climb out of her seat, she reaches for me. I do the same that I did with Lane, except Lucy doesn't try to run off, instead she links her fingers with mine and leads me in Lane's direction.

"Are you having fun, sweet girl?" I swing our arms, well, the best I can since she's barely above my knees and the height difference doesn't allow for much give in our arms.

"Bah."

"What?" I laugh, I still struggle to understand them.

"Bah." Her bottom lip pops out.

"Oh, you mean your sheep?" I reach into the diaper bag that's thrown over my shoulders and pull out her stuffed sheep. She doesn't leave the house without it, and since she can't say sheep, she just screams bah constantly.

"Bah!" She squeals in delight, yanking the sheep from my hand. She pulls it against her, snuggling it's head between her shoulder and chin as she squeezes with all her might.

"You better go play," I tell her, glancing at my watch. We've been here for a while, and they'll need to get home for dinner shortly.

Normally, I try to spend time with them on the weekends but since I told Tessa I'd take them to the park today, I left work a little early so I could bring them. She smiles up at me but trots off in the direction her brother just went.

The small park is gated, which is really nice when you bring two toddlers to the playground.

"Lou." I turn to the voice and see Tim Schaeder walking toward me.

"Tim, how are you?" I smile when he stops beside me.

Tim's changed over the last few years, he has a son now and it's matured him. Just like Kyle, although if he heard me comparing the two of them, he'd die.

He can't stand Tim.

In high school, right before I started dating Declan, I went on a date with Tim. There was nothing between us, it was one of the worst dates I've ever been on. By the end of the night, I was just ready to be home and forget the entire situation.

Tim had other plans and wanted a kiss but I wasn't into it. The next day, there were rumors all over school about how good of a lay I was for him. Tim and Declan never got along because of it and Kyle still holds a grudge against him to this day for it.

"I'm good." He looks over at the playground, pointing at his son. "Brought Connor out today, he's been at his mom's and I've missed the little guy." Connor's a cute little boy with bright blond hair and blue eyes, nearly the spitting image of his dad.

"How's that going?" I ask. I couldn't imagine being in their situation.

The two started dating and ended up pregnant right after, I don't even think they celebrated their two months before they were announcing their pregnancy. Somewhere down the line, they both realized they couldn't stand each other and split up. Now they share custody of Connor, and neither one of them can look at the other without wanting to throw up.

"Ah, it's going. It sucks honestly." He drops his head.

"I'm sorry." I look over at the kids playing. "I couldn't imagine."

"Yeah." He laughs, awkwardly. "So, I heard you're single now." My head snaps toward him.

"Damn, news travels fast." I chuckle, I had just had the conversation with Peter this morning before I went to work. It honestly went better than I thought it would, he wasn't upset... honestly, he barely said three words the entire time I was explaining how I felt. By the time I was finished, he asked if I was done and left.

"But, yeah. It was time, ya know?" I shrug my shoulders.

"I get it. His loss."

I nearly cringe at his words, because I know what's coming next.

"Well," he laughs, awkwardly scratching the back of his head. "I thought maybe that you and I could, um, get together sometime." And there it is.

"Listen," I turn to face him, taking a deep breath, "you and I have a past." I laugh. "A not so good past, and I think you've changed but I'm just not ready to jump back into anything. I've been hurt, and I'm not emotionally, physically, or mentally prepared to even entertain the idea of a night out with a guy."

"I figured as much." He smiles, but it doesn't reach his eyes. I've hurt his feelings and that makes me feel bad. "I just had to ask, and for the record, I'm sorry for what I did in high school. I was a dick and it wasn't fair for you."

"Thank you," I tell him before I look back at the kids and glance at my watch. "Well, it's almost time for me to get them back home."

"Yeah, I guess us too."

"Lucy, Lane," I yell, they both turn their heads before dropping the rocks in their hands and heading in our direction.

"Connor," Tim calls, except he won't come to him. "Well, I guess we aren't quite done after all." He laughs and starts walking in their direction.

"It was good seeing you, Tim," I call after him, grabbing the twins' hands.

"You, too." He smiles.

I wish that I could have found this version of Tim in high school, maybe things would have played out differently for us.

"Let's get you two home."

———

I'M exhausted when I walk into work the next day, but thank God it's Friday and the weekend is upon us. Peter moved all of his things out yesterday while I was at work and I haven't talked to him since. I don't know where he is staying or what his plans are, I just know I feel like I'm free.

I can breathe without having to answer to anyone. It's a strange feeling, especially after being in a relationship for so many years. My heart aches still, for the years lost and the amount of time I've let myself sit and be miserable for so long, and now it's time to find myself.

"Goodmorning," I step inside one of the patient rooms and greet the couple. "How are we doing today?"

"So far, so good. I'm starting to feel her move more," Autumn tells me, rubbing her hand over her swollen belly. Her husband sits beside her, a large smile on his face. They've been trying for years to have a baby and are finally the furthest they've ever been.

"Sleeping good still?" I wash my hands before moving over to the ultrasound machine.

"Sometimes. I take more naps than anything." She smiles at me.

"I sleep fine, thanks for asking," Her husband adds.

I chuckle. Ben has always been one of those guys that makes you laugh, with nearly everything he says.

"I'm glad to hear that," I tell him, turning my attention to the screen. "We're right at the thirty-four week mark. Getting closer." She lays back on the bed while I boot it up. I grab the gel and I'm about to warn her that it'll be a cool feeling but she cuts me off.

"I know, it'll be cold."

I nod, squirting it onto her bare stomach before grabbing the wand and smearing it around.

"Alright, let's see what we're measuring at today." I smile at the screen, the image appears and I turn the sound on so they can hear their sweet girl's heartbeat. It brings tears to Autumn's eyes every time. "Looks like you're still measuring ahead of schedule a little." I click a few buttons and make a few more measurements before I hit print and wipe the wand off.

I grab a few napkins to clean Autumn up but as always she takes them from me and does it herself, with the help of her husband. When I watch the two of them, they remind me of Declan and myself when we were younger. Not the pregnancy part, but the way that they move and work together.

My heart aches like it always does when I think of him. All the what if's coming back in full force. The day he broke up with me is etched into my mind and plays on repeat when he pops into my head. It's easy to remember the good times with him, but then they're quickly covered up by that one day. That one moment where he reacted without giving me any explanation about what I did.

The next day he was gone, he left town after he talked to me and as far as I know he hasn't been back. I see his mom occasionally but I avoid the topic of Declan Sanchez all together.

It's easier for me that way.

After I'm finished with Autumn, I head into another room where I have a vaginal ultrasound. This couple is early in their pregnancy, but she's been panicked and worried about her pregnancy since she found out so I told Talia to put them on the schedule for today.

They're my last appointment of the day, and for once I'm excited. I'll be leaving well before six o'clock tonight, and I'm actually not dreading it for the first time.

Their visit is quick, and once I'm finished up with them, I head to my office and finish all of the open charts I have. By the time five rolls around, I'm excited for the weekend and I'm completely caught up until Monday.

When I get home, it's quiet and dark. I flip the lights on and look around my house. Everything is still in its place after Peter left, because I owned everything except his clothes basically. He never paid for anything, practically living here for free. I paid for food, for the mortgage, for the car, for *everything*.

Just as I'm sitting down with a glass of wine, and getting ready to turn on the latest episode of *The Challenge*, my phone rings.

It's the hospital.

I frown, because I'm not on call this weekend but I answer it anyway, holding it against my ear. "Dr. Tucker."

"Hi, Doctor. I have a patient here that has completed paperwork and listed you as their obgyn. Her name is Autumn Baker." My heart drops and I start to move around my house, grabbing everything I'll need to head to the hospital. "I know you aren't on call this weekend but I just wanted to give you a call–"

"What's going on?" I ask.

"She's dialating." No, no, no. It's too early.

"I'm on my way." I don't end the call, I just shove the phone into my back pocket and grab my keys before rushing out the door. The hospital is about ten minutes from my house, which is also handy when I'm on call and there are emergency situations like this.

I break a few traffic laws on the way to the hospital, but I couldn't care less right now. I've been working with this couple for so long, I'm not risking the speed limit keeping me from getting to them.

Once I get inside, I meet with the on-call OBGYN and he explains that he has pushed Terbutaline but so far she hasn't had a reaction to it. The baby's heart rate has dropped twice before I got here and it isn't looking promising.

"We'll have to deliver," I tell him, he nods, handing the chart over to me.

I dress as quickly as I can before heading into the room to suit up the rest of the way. Autumn and Ben have already been made aware of what's happening and I'm sure she's sick over it all. Absolutely terrified of the unknown.

When I push the door to her room open, I see tears running down her face. "Hi, Autumn. How are we doing?" Her head lifts, and relief settles in her eyes. "I'm going to do everything I can." I look at her and she slowly nods. "She's going to be earlier than we like, but she's a fighter."

I move into position, letting the nurses move around me and do their jobs. My career would literally be nothing without these amazing people that do their jobs so well.

Nurses are amazing.

"Okay, Autumn. I'm going to need you to take a deep breath," I scoot my stool closer between her legs. I can see the baby crowning. "And then push down into your bottom, okay?"

She nods, looking over at her husband. He runs his hand over her forehead before bending and kissing her.

"Alright, three, two, one, push." As soon as I say the word, I hear her take a deep breath before pushing down like I said. The baby pushes a little more through the birth canal and she has a head full of dark hair. "Okay, Autumn. Great job, you're doing great," I say. "I need you to do it again for me. Ready?"

"No," she cries out. "I can't."

"Look at me." I raise slightly so she can see me. "You can do this, you are so brave and so strong." She looks me in the eyes before nodding slowly. "Ready?"

She nods.

"Three, two, one, push." She pushes again and I'm able to grab their babygirl and pull her free. I hand her off to one of the NICU nurses who deposits her small body into the incubator and wheels her out of the room.

"Go with her," Autumn tells Ben. "Make sure she's okay."

He looks from the door back to her, feeling torn on what he needs to do before she pushes him gently, forcing him to follow her.

I watch men struggle in that position quite often, and it makes me wonder how horrible it must be. To have to choose between your wife who is experiencing so many emotions and physically unable to be where she needs to be while having a newborn that's struggling to stay in this world and needs all the love and support they can get.

"Is she going to be okay?" Autumn asks me.

I want to tell her yes, that she has nothing to worry about but at this stage, you really don't know. Anything can happen. I've seen babies born with the best chances, only to take a turn for the worse.

"They're going to do everything that they can, Autumn. I promise you that." The fear in her eyes guts me. I want to take this away, give them a healthy baby girl. There was no sign of this when they were in my office earlier.

By the time I'm finished with Autumn, Ben is walking in with an update.

"She's stable," he tells her. "She's responding well so far. Her lungs aren't fully developed so they're doing all kinds of stuff but my mind was all over the place and I didn't get a lot of details."

"It's okay," she tells him. "They'll give us an update." She looks up at him. "Is she beautiful?"

"Like her mother," he tells her, bending forward and pressing his lips to hers.

"I'll give you both some time, if you need anything at all, have them page me." I tell them both.

"Thank you so much, Dr. Tucker." I smile before walking out the door.

When I get to my car, I call Tessa. I need someone to vent to.

6

DECLAN

"So, tell me, Declan. How is it being home?" Dr. Tinnin asks through the webcam.

I fucking hate doing sessions like this more than I do the in person ones. It feels awkward, even being somewhere that I'm completely comfortable, it feels strange. Like is he analyzing my childhood bedroom, looking at the mess of my sheets and how I didn't make the bed this morning?

"It's different," I tell him.

"What's different about it?"

"Well, when I pulled in, I immediately felt like shit," I answer truthfully.

"Why's that?" I can't see his hands, but I can tell he's writing something in that notepad he always uses.

"The house looked rough." I shrug my shoulders. "Like the driveway has overgrown with grass and a gutter is hanging off the side of the house."

"Okay, but why did that make you feel like shit?" he asks.

"Because it's my responsibility to take care of things like this for my mom, and I haven't been here for any of it."

"Who said it was your responsibility?"

I look him in the eyes. Is he serious?

"My father always told me I was the man of the house when he was gone. I let all of this fall apart because I was too stubborn to come back home and visit," I answer, running a hand over my face in frustration.

"But, Declan... do you live there?"

I frown at him. What?

"What?"

"Do you live there? Or do you live somewhere else."

"You already know the answer to that, Doc." And he does. He's a fucking therapist that works exclusively with military vets, he knows I've lived on base my entire career.

"I do, but I want to hear *you* say it." He smirks.

I want to throw my laptop. I hate that he's so fucking good at his job, because right now I know where he's going with this and I hate that he's making a break through and changing my thought process at the same fucking time.

"I live on the base."

"Exactly, so why do you feel responsible? Is your mother not capable of spraying round up or driving a nail through a gutter?"

My first instinct is to defend my mom, she shouldn't have to do any of this shit... but I also know where he's going with this and I hate that he's right.

Truth is, my mom is more than capable to do all the things here on her own but I know that she struggles with a lot of it now since Dad died and I left. She probably feels like there isn't a point to have the house looking as good as it used to anymore. Her joy died long ago.

"It's not," I mutter. "It's not my responsibility."

"Good." He smiles. "That's good. Granted, there is nothing wrong with you helping while you're there. It'll do you some good, keep your mind busy." He pauses, writing something down. "Have you seen Lou at all?"

I shake my head, I just got here and haven't left my mom's house other than to walk Gunnar around the neighborhood. Even then, it's at five in the morning when I do my runs so it isn't like I'm running into very many people.

"Have you thought about what that's going to be like when you do?" he questions, leaning back in his leather computer chair.

"Not really."

"You'll run into her at some point, Declan. I want you to be prepared for that moment. You're back home and on extended leave for a reason, we need to put all your demons to rest in order to get you back with your team."

"I understand."

"I won't clear you until I think you're ready," he warns.

"I understand, sir."

"Alright, good session today." He glances at the watch on his wrist. "Same time next week?"

"Sounds good."

"Have a good weekend, Declan. Get out of the house, do something. Don't let yourself drown in your thoughts." He smiles, says goodbye and then ends the Zoom meeting.

Leaving me to stare at myself and wonder how I was once a happy dude, and now I'm a miserable piece of shit.

———

"GUNNAR," I call, walking toward the front door of my mom's house with his leash in my hand.

"Where are you two heading?" Mom asks, smiling at me from her seat in the living room.

"Just for a walk, I need to clear my mind after that session with Dr. Tinnin."

She nods, taking a drink of her coffee. "Alright, be careful."

Pushing the door open, I let Gunnar run out first before shutting the door behind me. I don't hook his leash to him until we're nearly at the end of the driveway. He doesn't need a leash, but I know it makes people that pass by us feel better.

He's a big ass dog after all, larger than most German Shepherds. He looks like a giant bear, and scary as fuck until he licks you. Then he's just a big baby.

We walk in silence, as I look around my old neighborhood in the light of day. There's not much to see at five in the morning when it's still dark outside and the street lights don't work half the time.

"Declan?" I cringe as soon as I hear the voice. "Declan Sanchez? Is that you?" Followed by a giggle. Gunnar halts next to me, and I really wish this was one of those moments where he wasn't a well trained duty dog and would bolt in the opposite direction and pull me with him.

Turning around, I see Jillian Baker walking toward me in a matching Adidas windbreaker set. She looks like a giant piece of bubble gum with the light pink color reflecting from her pale skin. I have to choke back the laugh that nearly bubbles out.

"Jillian, hi." I smile, trying to be polite. My mom would kick my ass if I was anything but.

She was a bitch in high school, to anyone and everyone. Except for me.

I knew she had a crush on me, which is why she was such a bitch to Lou all the time. When Tim Schaefer spread those rumors about Lou being an easy lay, Jillian jumped right on board.

Jealousy is an ugly trait, which is one of the reason's I never found Jillian attractive.

"How have you been?" She stops a step away from me, her arm extends toward me and for a second I think she's going to shake my hand but instead she squeezes the muscle of my forearm. "Gosh, you're so strong now."

"Ha." I awkwardly shift away from her and watch as her arm drops to her side. Gunnar makes a noise and her eyes move from mine down to him.

"Oh my gosh, what is that?" she asks, jumping back a step.

"Um, a dog." I frown at her.

"Oh, right. I know that... but like is he your dog or something?"

"Yeah," I draw out. Who else's dog would I be randomly walking?

"Oh, cute." She's obviously scared or disgusted, maybe a little of both but she reaches out and pats the top of his head so quick, I don't even think Gunnar feels it. "So," she stands back to her full height and shifts so she's standing on my other side, the one farthest from Gunnar, "since you're back in town, we should get together. Catch up. You can buy me a drink."

Damn, is this what women are like now?

"Yeah, maybe," I answer, not having any truth in the words as they leave my lips.

I don't want to go out with Jillian. She was never my type, and her hair is the wrong shade of blonde for me. Not to mention her eyes are brown, and I'm only interested in one beautiful shade of blue.

"Okay, well, here's my number." She holds out a business card. Her face is plastered to the front of it and her contact information next to it. I look it over, trying to figure out what business she's working for but then it hits me...

This is literally the card she hands out for people to call her. I laugh slightly, unable to control it and when she frowns I almost feel bad.

"Thanks for this." I hold it up between us. "Have a good day, Jillian."

I tug on Gunnar's leash, and he falls into step beside me, not giving Jillian another glance.

"Oh, you're so welcome," she shouts. "See you soon for our date."

Ah, fuck.

That's the last thing I need.

7

LOU

MY EYES ARE FILLING with tears from what I've just had to do. It never gets easier, no matter how long I do his job, it's always hard.

I've delivered enough babies to know this is common and a risk that everyone has, even when the pregnancy is smooth sailing... it can still happen.

Glancing at the screen of my car, I hit the favorites tab and tap Tessa's picture. I don't want to be alone right now.

"Hey," she answers on the first ring. When I don't answer her immediately she asks, "What's wrong?" Her voice changing from the upbeat sound it was to being full of concern.

"I just delivered a baby," I pause, dreading the word I'm about to say. "*Early*."

"Oh no." I can hear my brother in the background asking what's wrong. "Where are you?"

"I'm heading home now," I tell her.

"Get ready, I'm coming to get you. You need a night out," she says.

"We just had one," I remind her. "Like two nights ago."

"I don't care, Kyle owes me plenty of nights out."

I can tell she's looking at my brother by the way she says it. And knowing him, he probably isn't arguing with her. Whatever Tessa wants, Tessa gets.

"Okay. See you in a bit."

We end the call, and I remind myself how blessed I am to have my family and friends.

I drive to my house, listening to the radio the entire way, trying to get the sinking feeling in my gut of that sweet baby girl out. This is the worst part about my job, not being able to do anything when a baby is born and out of your control.

I waited at the hospital as long as I could, but sadly it's out of my control now. Momma was good, healthy in every way, but there was nothing I could do at the hospital for that baby girl tonight so I told myself I needed to leave. She's in the care of some of the best pediatric doctors, and I'm just an OBGYN.

When I pull into my drive, Tessa is already parked in front of my garage. I hit the button and watch as the door slides open and she climbs out of her car. Pulling my car in, I park and climb out. She's already there when I turn, wrapping her arms around me.

"You okay?" she whispers against my ear.

"I will be, I just hate this part of it."

She pulls away from me. "I get it."

I let her go and walk inside to change. "Kyle was okay with taking another night off so we could go out?" I step inside my kitchen and drop my purse on the island.

"Yeah, I think he enjoys having alone time with the kids. He doesn't get it very often." She smiles at me, following me through the house. I look over at what she's wearing, skinny jeans and a loose sweater.

I'll wear something similar. God knows I have plenty of clothes that don't really get to see the light of day since I'm mostly in scrubs or professional clothes covered with a white jacket.

"Is it just us?"

"I texted all the girls. Chloe couldn't come out tonight, she didn't really give a reason and I didn't push too hard. Nicole said she'd meet us there, but I haven't heard back from Talia yet."

I walk into my closet, leaving Tessa sitting on my bed so I can change. Within ten minutes, I'm dressed and in Tessa's car heading toward Arrow.

When we walk inside, you can tell it's a Friday night. It's packed. Most of the tables are occupied, but one says *Reserved* and when I see Tessa walking toward it, I know this was my brother's doing.

Nights like this always have me down, but I'm so thankful for Tessa. Since she and my brother got together, she's just been my go to person. We clicked instantly and I don't know what I'd do without her now.

"Hey, bitches." Nicole walks in, dropping her purse on the table before sitting beside me. "Rough day?"

I nod.

"Well, let's take your mind off of it." Her grin is wide before she pushes out of her seat and heads for the bar. Talia walks up behind me, startling me.

"You okay?" she asks, hanging her purse on the back of her chair and rubbing her hand over my back.

Since she came out with us the other day, she's been

included in all of our group texts and is quickly becoming one of my good friends.

"Yeah, I'll be fine. It just sucks."

She rubs her hand over my back for a second before climbing into her seat. A few seconds later, two shot glasses are placed in front of me, courtesy of Nicole.

"Let's drink, babes. It's Friday night and my kids are with my parents, which means I don't have to wake up at the ass crack of dawn." She holds her glass to the center of the table and looks around.

"Cheers," Tessa says, clinking her small glass against hers.

Talia and I do the same before tipping the brown liquid back. My face screws up when the bitter taste slides down my throat.

"Whew!" I shout, still feeling the burn in my chest.

"Hot Damn," Nicole looks over at me. I should have known by the cinnamon taste and because it's... "My favorite drink." She takes the words right out of my mouth. If Nicole is in charge, the drinks will always be some form of cinnamon.

After our second shot, the song changes and we all head toward the dance floor. *Side Effects* by Ty Dolla $ign is blaring through the speakers. We all have our arms above our head as we sway to the beat of the song. I let all the heartache from the night up to this point leave my body.

A few girls join us on the dance floor, forming a large circle while we all dance. Guys are standing to the side, staring as we shake our bodies. Normally, I'd be shy and reserved but with all the changes that have taken place recently and the stress of the evening, I let loose.

After a few more songs, my legs are about to give out so I tell the girls I'm heading back to our table for a break. If these girls' nights keep happening, I'm going to have to start working out to make sure I can last longer than a couple songs. My thighs are killing me from my failed attempts at twerking.

Tony brings a cold beer and sits it in front of me, letting me know someone from the back table ordered it for me before heading back to the bar. When I look over, the man raises his glass to me before turning his attention back to his group. More people have come in tonight, and every table is taken including each spot at the bar.

"Didn't expect to see you here tonight." An arm drops to the table beside me, a beer in their hand. When I look up, I see Tim, dressed in a button down with the sleeves rolled partly up his forearms. He smells good, like some fancy cologne but it's not my favorite.

No, I haven't smelt that smell in fifteen years.

"I guess I could say the same about you, especially since it's my brother's bar," I point out but smile at him.

It's no secret that the two of them don't like each other, and I'm not sure they'll ever get along, even though their kids are fairly close in age and will more than likely go to school together. He laughs, the sound deep and I don't know if it's because I've been drinking or what but it's sexy.

What the fuck am I doing? No, Lou. Bad, Lou.

"My son's with his mom tonight, I didn't want to be alone," he admits.

My stomach falls with his admission, and I start wondering how he does it. I don't know his baby momma, but I've heard stories about the two of them. It's similar to Tessa and Kyle's story in a way, except there was no happily ever after there. Everything I've been told is that he's a damn good dad and the mom is always wanting more. They're constantly in court battles, fighting for custody or more child support.

"Ah." I nod my head slowly, lifting my drink to his. "I can understand that."

He looks from the dance floor to me. "You here for girls' night?" He chuckles.

"Yeah, I had a rough night with a work situation and needed to blow off some steam." I shrug. "It's working." I laugh, thinking about the night so far as I look back over at the dance floor where my friends are attempting to do some type of dance that I've never seen.

"Good," He looks into my eyes and shifts closer to me. "Good."

The girls come over to the table then, breaking the look Tim has and I'm thankful, because I'm not really liking this pull I have to Tim right now. "Tim, how are you?" Nicole asks, but she doesn't give him time to respond. "Making up lies about teenage girls still?" she smirks.

"That was a long time ago, Nicole. Lou and I have moved on." He looks at me, and he's right.

I've let go of a lot of the shit from my past, and him apologizing makes it easier to do so. I don't want to be one of those people that live for years holding grudges against people.

But yet, here I am, still holding hate for a man I once loved with everything in me. Declan is still at the top of my shit list, and I don't think he'll ever recover from that spot. But at least it's easier without him being here.

Nicole looks over to me, brows raised.

I nod, confirming what Tim's just said to be true.

"Well, damn. Alright then." She takes another drink of her beer and any tension that was present is long gone and our care free fun night is back in place.

Tony keeps bringing drinks, Tim has bought us all a round of shots and toasted to a peace offering between us. I laughed while Nicole rolled her eyes, but she still downs the drink before heading back to the dance floor.

Tessa is enjoying herself tonight, she and Nicole have remained tied at the hip since they're both married. Talia has caught the attention of a hot brunette with eyes that will make any woman melt. He's escorted her to the dance floor multiple times and she's even hinted at going home with him tonight. Tim is at the bar, talking to a few guys I recognize but can't place them while I continue to nurse my beer at the table.

The crowd is thick, even for nearly midnight you can't find an empty table in the room. I look over where Nicole is dancing, her eyes slide to mine but widen for a moment.

"Lou." The deep timbre of that voice causes my blood to run cold and my body locks up. It's a voice I've tried to forget for the last fifteen years. Only I couldn't forget it no matter how hard I try.

But can we talk about the damn irony of this situation? Of course his ass would come back... when I'm moving on and finding myself for the first time in my life. Of course he'd come back when I feel like things will start looking up and I'll be able to smile for the first time in years where it isn't forced.

Of fucking course he would.

I slowly turn, bringing my eyes up to the man in front of me. His hair is short, much shorter than how he used to wear it. There's a slight scruff along his jaw making him look older. His skin has a deep tanned complexion, one that I know he could only get from overseas. His green eyes bore into mine, fifteen years of emotion passing between us.

Never in a million years did I think I'd be standing in front of him again. Even living in the same place all my life, I figured he was long gone and wouldn't be returning.

At least not long enough for us to have a run in. And for fifteen years, it worked. So why now? Why the change?

What did I ever do to deserve this shit?

"How have you been?" he asks, shifting his feet slightly and shoving his hands into his worn jeans.

Jeans that fit him *so* damn good that it makes me forget why I can't stand him. His t-shirt stretches across his muscles, showing every indention of his body against the thin fabric. He's not the boy that left here that day all those years ago, he's a rock solid man standing in front of me now. "Lou?" His voice shocks me back to reality.

"How have I been?" I laugh, how have I been?

Well, let's see, I've spent fifteen years getting over you, half of those years were with another man that should've been you, and now I'm single, in a bar, getting wasted. Yeah, I'd say I've been just fucking fine.

I don't say that of course, because I don't want him to know how miserable I've been without him all this time. "I've been good." I smile, trying my damndest to stay strong and not show that I'm shaking on the inside.

"Good." He looks down at my hand as I lift my beer to my lips, scanning my fingers for what I'm assuming is a ring. "You're not married?"

I shake my head, panic starting to set in. Out of the

corner of my eye, I see Tim walking toward me and before I can even think straight, I'm latching onto his arm and pulling him against me. The smell of his cologne is no longer appealing because I feel the need to throw up, but I've got to do something.

I'll blame this all on the alcohol tomorrow, but right now I need an escape and Tim is going to give it to me. He owes me at least that much.

"No," I say, wrapping my arm around Tim's waist.

Declan looks between the two of us, nearly stumbling back a step when he sees the man with his hand snaking around my own waist.

"Tim and I didn't really see the point in getting married." I shrug, looking up at Tim with begging eyes to play along. I'll castrate him if he doesn't. He frowns before catching on to what I'm doing.

"Yeah, man." Tim shrugs. "No point," he says. He sits his beer on the table, reaching a hand out between the two of them, but keeping his other firmly planted on my waist. "How've you been?" he asks Declan.

I'm expecting something far different to come out of Declan's mouth than what he says.

"Good, just moved back home."

Fuck me.

Moved back home?

As in permanently?

"That's good. Your mom doing okay?" Tim asks.

I'm thankful his arm hasn't left my side, it's probably the only thing holding me up right now. Between the alcohol swarming my brain and the scent of Declan's signature cologne, I'm drowning.

I've missed that smell, and when it hit me I nearly

tumbled to the ground, feeling my heart crack all over again.

"Yeah, she's doing good."

I excuse myself from both of them, grabbing my purse from the table and heading in the direction of Nicole who is already meeting me halfway.

"What the fuck?" she says.

"I need to leave." I look at her. "*Now.*"

She nods and gestures for Tony, we're all in the back of his car within a few minutes heading toward my house.

What a fucked up night.

8
DECLAN

"How've you been?" Tim asks me.

I'm having a hard time concentrating on him because all I see is his hand on her waist and it fucking makes me want to murder the little shit.

"Good, just moved back home," I tell him, flicking my eyes over Lou.

Goddamn she looks good. Her jeans are painted on her body, with the front of her loose sweater tucked in at the button.

Her blonde hair hasn't changed at all since the last time I saw her. When I realized she didn't have a ring on her finger, I was so fucking relieved she wasn't with that douche bag I'd seen her in the store with a few years ago.

I also don't miss the way her eyes widen when I tell them I just moved back home.

"That's good. Your mom doing okay?" Tim asks, his arm tightening around her slightly.

I don't know how much she's had to drink tonight, but I swear she sways a little.

"Yeah, she's doing good," I tell them.

Lou excuses herself, grabbing her purse and heading toward where her friends are. I recognize Nicole, but I don't know the others. She says something to Nicole that has them all grabbing their things while Nicole waves for the bartender and they all exit through the back door.

Tim doesn't even notice she's left, he's still in conversation with me about something. I'm not even listening to him, I watch Lou until the door slams shut. I want to go after her, demand that she talk to me but I know I can't do that. It'll only make things worse.

"Let me buy you a drink," he offers.

I follow him to the bar.

Tim seems like he's grown up a lot since high school, and clearly Lou has forgiven him for the shit he's done since she's *dating* him.

Granted, I'm not one-hundred percent sold on that yet, considering she didn't even tell her man she was leaving and he hasn't said two words about her since she disappeared.

"So, you and Lou, huh?" I ask.

"What?" he frowns at me, and then almost as if he's remembering he answers. "Oh, yeah. Crazy right?"

"The craziest," I say, sarcastically.

The bartender approaches, he's a younger dude but seems to know his shit. When Tim rattles off two drink orders and he gets to work, filling the glasses from whatever they have on tap.

"What's been going on around town?" I ask, curious to see what I've missed out on.

"Same ole shit. Except I have a kid." He looks over at me, a smile on his face.

"No shit?"

He nods, digging in his pocket for his phone. He taps the screen and a picture of a little boy that looks identical to him is the background.

"He's cute. Congrats."

"Thanks, man." He smiles at his phone before he locks it and puts it back in the pocket.

"So, you and Lou have a kid?" I ask the question I don't really want the answer to.

"Fuck no." He laughs. "I wish."

I cringe at his words. Me too.

"My ex is fucking psychotic and every day is something new that she wants done or hates about our arrangement. It's a fucking disaster, but he's worth it."

"I get that." I take the drink that's slid in front of me and lift it to my lips.

Turning on my barstool, I take in the look of the bar. It's nice, nicer than I expected this old place to be. It's one of the oldest buildings in town, but they've remodeled it well and clearly it's everyone's favorite spot.

"I ran into Jillian Baker earlier today, what's going on with her?"

"Man, that bitch hasn't changed at all since high school." He laughs. "I'm actually surprised she isn't out tonight, scoping out her next victim."

"She seems the same."

"You have no idea." He chuckles. "Did she give you one of her cards?"

"She did."

"Is that not some crazy shit? I bet every dude in this bar has one of them. She's still single, but she makes her way around town." He shakes his head. "I wouldn't go near her with a ten foot pole, my man."

"I didn't plan on it," I admit.

"Good, she's clingy as fuck."

I can see that, she was that way in school, too.

A few girls walk over to us, one not hiding the fact that she's interested in me at all.

Know what the problem is? She's not blonde, she doesn't have blue eyes, and her name isn't fucking Lou.

I excuse myself, thank Tim for the drink and head for the door.

I'll be able to tell my therapist that I got out of the house, enjoyed a chat with someone I went to school with, didn't get into any fights, and came home sober.

9

LOU

"WHAT IN THE ACTUAL FUCK?" Nicole waves her arms around while climbing onto my couch and reaching over for a piece of pizza we picked up on the way home.

"So, wait, fill me in," Tessa says, grabbing her own slice.

Talia didn't make it home with us, she decided she was going to have a night with the hottie she met earlier. And I honestly don't blame her for that a bit.

"That tall, dark, and fucking handsome as hell man at the bar was none other than Lou's ex, *Declan*." Nicole forces the pizza into her mouth, taking a large bite and I watch in disbelief at how she fits so much food in her mouth at once.

"Don't get that on my fucking couch." I point at her, earning me a middle finger in return.

"He's the one that left you without any explanation?" Tessa stares at me, waiting for an answer.

I've told her a little bit about what happened between Declan and me, but I'm sure Kyle filled in any of the blanks I left out.

"The one and only." I shrug my shoulders and grab my own slice, looking down at the pepperoni. I really don't have an appetite after running into Declan tonight, but if I don't eat something to absorb some of this alcohol in me, I'll feel like death tomorrow.

"What the hell is he doing back?" Nicole looks at me between bites. "Like why now? It's been fucking fifteen years."

"How the hell am I supposed to know?" I take a bite, thinking of the reasons he could be here. "I wish I did," I say while chewing, really classy looking I'm sure.

"You didn't ask?"

I shake my head no.

"What the ever-loving-fuck."

"What?" I shrug. "I was in shock." I glare at her. "What would you do if the love of your life walked back in after fifteen years?" She stares at me. "Besides, I was too busy pretending Tim was my fucking boyfriend to think about anything else." I slap a palm to my forehead.

"Shut up." Her eyes widen before she falls back onto the couch in a fit of laughter. The maniacal sound makes me cover my ears. "Holy shit, you didn't."

"I sure the fuck did." I shake my head, because even I can't believe I did what I did tonight. I just wanted him to know that he didn't have control over me anymore, even though he still one hundred percent controls my emotions. That much was proven tonight. But, I didn't want him to see how miserable I really am. I'm in my thirties and single, never been married, no kids. All I do is work and hang out with my brother and his kids.

What a life.

Tim just happened to be at the wrong place at the

wrong time. Thank God he went along with my theatrics. I was seriously nervous that he wasn't going to catch on and give the entire thing away. Whatever was going through Declan's mind was probably comical, because when he left town, I couldn't stand Tim and wouldn't have gone near him with a ten foot pole... but that's behind us and he's apparently my fake boyfriend.

"Wow." Nicole laughs. "And Tim went along with it?"

"Oh my gosh, I was so damn nervous that he wouldn't understand what I was trying to do and ruin the entire thing." I take another bite. "Then I would have really stepped in it."

"Honey, I don't think you could step in it anymore if you tried." Nicole laughs.

"Give her a chance," Tessa adds.

I just glare at my friends before rolling my eyes.

We talk for hours before we all pass out on the couch, the last thing that runs through my mind is Declan and that awful day fifteen years ago.

———

I WOKE up when the girls got up this morning and went home. Hopped in the shower to get the stench of the beer and bar from my skin before I climbed back into my bed for a long nap.

The night was very much needed but my big ass mouth saying I was dating Tim was not...

Now I'm laying in bed, fully dressed for lunch with my brother but thoughts from that day are playing on repeat in my mind.

I hate that after all this time, he can still bring tears to my eyes from the pain of him walking away. I'll never understand it, I still don't understand it.

I thought we had everything.

Everything together. That's what he would always say.

We had talked about our future and what we were going to do. I knew that the military was something that was always on the backburner, but he had always talked about attending school to become something of himself. Not that the military wouldn't give him that, it was just that the military was his father's way of life, and Declan wanted more.

Which is why nothing made sense when I found out he had joined.

My head falls to the side, staring at the clock on my nightstand. I have ten minutes until I'm meeting my brother at a diner down from his bar to eat lunch. It's one of my favorite parts of the week, our regularly scheduled lunch date that we've been doing for the past few years. It's never the same day each week, but we make sure to schedule one in.

Grabbing my phone, I see a message from Tim and groan. How fucking embarrassing.

Tim: So, wanna explain what the hell happened last night?

Me: I am so sorry!! I don't know what came over me.

Tim: Haha. It's okay. I was confused as fuck at first.

Me: Trust me, I was confused the entire time.

Tim: Where'd you disappear to?

Me: I freaked. Grabbed the girls and hauled ass out the backdoor.

Tim: Ah. That makes sense. Shit, I didn't even notice you left until Declan said something about it. I guess I'm a shitty boyfriend.

I laugh, if only he knew how fast I got out that door last night. I had this sinking feeling that Declan was going to follow me. The girls were probably wondering why the hell I kept looking over my shoulder but they didn't say anything, even when I nearly fell on my face.

Me: It's okay, we had only been dating for like five minutes at the time.

Tim: Haha, I guess you're right. Are you busy today?

Me: Yeah, heading out to lunch with my brother. But, thanks for covering for me, I seriously appreciate it.

Tim: No worries, I owe you that much at least.

I don't bother texting back, instead hurrying to get ready to meet Kyle. I'm starving and my head is pounding.

Thoughts of Declan are swarming in my head while I drive to the diner, memories from the past I can't seem to keep buried any longer. I park my car along the side of the diner, and climb out to walk toward where my brother has parked his truck. He climbs out, turning toward me with a smile as he shuts the door.

"Hey." He smiles, pulling me in for a hug.

I relax against him, letting the comfort of my brother calm my nerves.

"I'm starving."

When he pulls away, it's almost like my blanket of calmness disappears. I follow him inside, staying quiet as we find our way to our normal seat and the waitress takes our drink orders.

"So," he pauses, "you going to tell me what happened last night or..." He smirks.

It's a look that he's perfected over the last ten years or so but still irritates the shit out of me when he does it.

Fucking Tessa... I knew she'd spill it to him as soon as she got home.

"What do you know?" I laugh, leaning forward in my seat and resting my elbows on the edge of the table. I take a deep breath, and blow it out slowly while I wait for him to answer.

"I know that Declan's back in town." His smirk disappears and he stares at me. "Tessa told me this morning."

I groan, shaking my head slightly and rubbing my hands along my face in a nervous attempt to hide from his glare. "I haven't seen him in fifteen years."

"I know." He tilts his head slightly, trying to gauge what type of emotion I'm feeling. And to be honest, I'm not even sure what I'm feeling. I'm hurt, I'm angry, I'm down right fucking broken. "Did he speak to you?"

"He asked how I was." I shrug, trying not to go any further into the events of the night.

"And?"

I roll my eyes. He already knows.

"Then I let him think that fucking Tim and I were together, which we are not." I hold my hand up to him. "Let me just clarify that right now." He stares at me as if to say *go on*. "Then the two of them got to talking and I bolted out the employee door."

"Fucking Tim? Of all people?" he scoffs. "Have you lost your fucking mind?"

"I panicked." My voice raises slightly, so I look around the diner to make sure no one is listening and I'm not causing a scene. "I panicked," I say again, this time quieter as I turn my attention back to Kyle. "He was the *last* person I expected to run into last night, and in your bar of all places."

He shakes his head, picking up the menu in front of him. Which is only a way to avoid the conversation while he gets his own emotions under control, Kyle orders the exact same burger every single time we come here.

Kyle hates Declan, with a passion. Which hurts, because at one point in time, they were so close. When we dated, I often wondered if Declan liked my brother more than he liked me. They spent so much of their time together back then, even though they were in separate grades.

"How long is he here for?"

I shrug again, while Kyle stares at me as if he doesn't believe me.

"He's home for a while." I admit, watching as he rolls his eyes.

"Fuck," he mumbles while the waitress sets our drinks down in front of us, Kyle thanks the girl and orders his typical burger like I knew he would before returning to the conversation. I choose the same, needing to fill my stomach with whatever carbs I can get.

"So, Tim?"

I groan at his question. I knew he'd bring it up.

"What about him?"

"Anything going on between the two of you?" I shake my head. "You sure?"

"Yes, I'm fucking sure," I whisper yell at him.

It's a thing. You know when you want to scream at someone for thinking something so off the wall but you can't because you're surrounded by people and that would cause a scene... that's when you whisper yell.

I pull the wrapper from my straw and shove it into my drink before bringing it to my lips. "He's the last person I'd be interested in. Even though everything happened *years* ago, I still don't like him for it. But he apologized a few days ago and I forgave him."

"What? When?"

"At the park the other day when I had the kids with me." His eyes bounce between mine. "He was there with his son, he apologized and I felt like it was sincere."

"I still don't fucking like him." Kyle crosses his arms over his chest, and I swear to you it's the same little boy that would pout every single time he didn't get his way when we were younger.

"Who *do* you like?" I ask, raising a brow.

"No one." He smirks.

I shake my head. The mood is lighter now and I'm thankful for it.

"Don't let Declan being back in town fuck with everything you have going right now, okay?"

"With what? I'm single, old as fuck, and have no kids." I chuckle. "Yeah, not much to fuck with there."

"I'm serious, Lou. I love you, and I don't want to see you hurt like that again." His words hit me in the chest, and for the first time I think about how it must have made everyone else in our house feel. I let myself slip into a deep depression once Declan left town. At that point, I didn't even want to live anymore. I thought my entire world was over after he walked away, and it honestly felt that way in the moment.

My mom was checking on me twenty-four-seven, but all

I did was lay in bed. I skipped meals, I lost weight, I didn't want to leave for college. But it was my brother who changed my thought process when he came into my room that day and reminded me of my worth.

"You deserve more than this, Lou. If he can't see that, that's on him. Not you. You did nothing wrong here, remember that. Don't let him ruin you, and don't let him be the cause of you doing something that you'll later regret."

His words still speak to me anytime I'm struggling with life.

Who knew his little ass would be so wise in a moment of need. Although, I can't tell him that because he'd never let me live it down that it was him who pulled me from that dark spot. I can't let him think he has that much clout.

"I love you," I tell him.

By the time lunch is over, my mind keeps replaying the vision of the boy who stole my heart and never really gave it back.

The couple that was supposed to make it, but sadly crumbled.

10

DECLAN

SEEING Lou was a surprise for me.

I wasn't expecting to see her, I didn't think a bar like that would be her scene. She wasn't much for partying when we were together in high school, aside from the average bonfire we'd throw. Other than that, she didn't do much of anything. She watched a lot of nursing shows back then, she was hooked on *Grey's Anatomy* when it first came out.

I wonder if she became a nurse? That's what she always wanted to do once school ended. When I left here fifteen years ago, she was getting ready to start nursing school and I was excited for her. She's probably an amazing nurse, she always cared so much for people.

Rubbing my hands over my face, I swing my legs to the side of my bed, connecting with a sleeping Gunnar on the floor. I bend, scratching behind his ears before standing and pull a pair of shorts on. The smell of bacon floats through the air, leading my stomach straight to the kitchen where my mom is in front of the stove.

"There's my boy." That voice doesn't come from my mom.

I turn to look at the table, my aunt sits with her legs crossed and a cigarette hanging from her fingers.

"My goodness, you're a man now." She laughs, waving me over.

"Hi, Aunt B." I walk around the table, bending to hug her. "When are you going to get rid of those things?" I ask, pulling back and gesturing to the cigarette in her hand.

I hate them, even when I was little I used to lecture her on the dangers of smoking and how it takes years off her life. She didn't care though, she'd smile, tell me to never pick one up and light her own.

"Oh," she swats me away, "these are my breathing treatments. You know that." She winks as I lean around my mom and kiss her cheek before sitting across from my aunt at the table. "Tell me, how have you been?" She looks at me. "You're huge now." She gestures to my arms.

"I work out a lot." I lean back in the chair, listening to the squeak beneath me and mentally remind myself to look at this later to make sure it doesn't need to be tightened. There's a growing list in my head of things I need to get done around here, and I need to start on them soon. "How have you been?"

"Oh, you know. Keeping the nights hot." She laughs, a deep laugh that gives away how many years she's been smoking.

My aunt is still wild at heart. The type that enjoys her nights out and refuses to settle down with one man, which is why she doesn't have any kids. Because raising a child alone was never on her agenda.

"The nights hot, huh? You ain't been dragging my momma out with you, have you?"

She shrugs.

"Momma!" I turn my attention to my mom as I say it, acting appalled by what I've just learned.

In all honesty, I'm glad my mom's getting out of the house and enjoying herself. Even if it isn't very often, at least I know she's living. Just the thought alone makes me smile.

"Oh, hush. You know your aunt couldn't drag me out if she tried, those days are long behind me."

Well, I guess if she isn't out running the streets I can at least take pride in the fact that she's still smart enough not to tangle up in everything Aunt B gets herself into. She plates a few strips of bacon before shoveling half the plate full of eggs. It reminds me of when I was a teenager, I ate more than both of my parents combined back then.

"Here." Her hand runs over my shoulder as she sits the plate in front of me.

"So, Aunt B., where have you been keeping the nights hot?" I ask, between shoving a fork full of eggs in my mouth. One thing I have missed continuously over the last decade is my momma's cooking. There's nothing else like it.

"Arrow. You been yet?"

Arrow?

"Actually, I was there last night." My mind flashes back to the night, seeing Lou for the first time. Watching as she wrapped her arm around Tim, of all people. Regardless, she looked so fucking beautiful. Seeing her, even if it wasn't planned and she wasn't where I'd prefer her to be, it was like breathing fresh air for the first time in fifteen years.

My heart was beating faster than it did any time I was overseas. I just wonder what was going through her head? Scratch that, I probably don't want to know the twelve different ways she tortured me in her mind last night... I'm good.

"You know Kyle Tucker owns that bar?" my aunt says, his name catches my attention. "He's done a real nice job, too. Lou comes in for lunch sometimes. Have you seen her yet?"

My mom smacks my aunt in the shoulder, fixing her with a look. My aunt's face scrunches up before realization of what she's just asked sets in.

"Oh, honey. I'm sorry. I didn't think." She reaches across the table to squeeze my hand.

"It's fine." I wave her off. "I didn't know Kyle owned it though."

"Yeah, he's had it a while." She smiles, but it doesn't reach her eyes. I know she feels bad about bringing Lou up. "Did you know she bought the clinic?"

I raise my brows.

"She was Doc's right hand for a while, he didn't have anyone to hand it down to so he let Lou buy it when he retired."

"I didn't know that either." Hearing that makes my chest swell, knowing that Lou has done so well for herself. But then it hits me, that same pain I've felt for years because I've missed out on all of that for her.

"Bethany, I need your help with something." My mom walks toward the hallway. "I bought a new dress and want to get your opinion on it."

I chuckle while my Aunt B. stands, following behind my mom while I finish my breakfast in silence. My mom always tries to fix everything, and I love her for it. But truthfully, even if Aunt B. hadn't brought Lou up, I'd still be thinking about the girl that owns my heart.

I STOP outside the door that faces the corner of the street, taking a deep breath before I muster up the courage to push it open. Coming here is a risk, but it needs to be done.

When I step inside, the overhead lights are on making it brighter than it was last night, taking my eyes a second to adjust. A few employees are working on cleaning up some tables, while others move around stocking things behind the bar.

My eyes scan over the open room until they land on the man I came to see. I haven't seen him in fifteen years either. Seems to be the trend with me and everyone here. At one point he was my best friend, we weren't the same age, but when Lou and I started dating we were always together.

He's standing at the end of the bar, flipping through some papers while he taps a few keys on a calculator. He's bigger than in high school, and looks like he takes weights seriously nowadays.

"Can I help you?" a voice beside him says.

I don't look at them. My eyes remain trained on Kyle. He's the one I'm here to see, no one else. His eyes dart to the person next to him before slowly turning his head in my direction. When he realizes someone is in his bar, a slight smile appears before he narrows his eyes at me and that smile falls just as quickly as it appeared.

He looks really thrilled to see me. This should be fun.

His lip curls in disgust as he turns his body to face me. He looks back over to his employee before dropping his pen to the bar and taking a few steps toward me. "What the fuck are you doing here?" His voice is laced with venom, he's not happy I'm here, but I didn't expect anything less.

"I just want to talk." I hold my hands up, trying to show him that I'm here in peace. "I—"

"I don't fucking care about what you have to say. Get the fuck out of my bar." He crosses his arms and stares me dead in the eyes.

"Kyle."

He turns away from me, shaking his head as he walks back toward where he was standing at the bar.

"Kyle!" My voice raises louder than I expected it to.

He halts, midstep before looking over at his employee and gesturing for them to head to the back of the bar. Kyle still doesn't turn around.

"It's not what you think."

His shoulders shake with silent laughter before he turns. The man in front of me is not the Kyle I remember, but I should have expected him to be considering it's been so long.

"Not what I think?" He shakes his head. "I think you fucking bailed on my sister, who loved you so much, more than you fucking deserved." He steps closer to me, a finger pointed toward my chest. "I think you're a fucking coward and whatever the fuck you were dealing with was a cop out for you to leave her." His words trigger something inside me.

Is that what they think? That I wanted to leave her and that was my way of getting out?

Is that what she thinks?

"You don't have a clue what you're fucking talking about." I step in his face, crowding him until our foreheads are nearly touching. Rage builds inside me. "Don't talk about something that you don't fucking know."

"Get the fuck out of here with that shit." We're so close I can feel the anger rolling off of him. "Do you know what it's like to almost lose your sister? To watch her whither away in front of you?" His chest bumps mine.

Of course I don't, I'm an only child but I know all about fucking loss.

"Do you? Because I fucking did. She was so fucking depressed after you up and left her. Without a fucking explanation as to why."

"I had no choice!" I shout back, working hard to contain my emotions. "I had no choice but to do what I did. You don't understand and you probably never will, Kyle."

"Fuck you." He shakes his head. "*Fuck. You.*"

"No, fuck you," I snap back. "I'm back in town, and I'm going to make things right with Lo—" I don't get the chance to finish what I'm saying. His fist comes out of nowhere, connecting with my jaw. I fall backwards, landing on my ass in front of him. The pain from his punch tingles along my jaw. Slowly, I move to stand and look him in the eyes. He looks almost pained that he hit me, and that's something I can't decipher. I wipe at the back of my jeans before facing him once again. "I didn't know how to deal with my dad dying." I run my hand over my jaw, trying to soothe the ache that's forming. "I didn't want Lou to end up like my mother, always waiting for the car to pull in and tell her that I was dead. I couldn't do that to her, Kyle. She deserved more, she deserved better than what I could give her."

He doesn't say anything, just stares at me while I speak so I continue. "I was checked out of our relationship long before that day. I couldn't process everything that was happening and before I knew it, I was enlisted with a ship out date."

Kyle's eyes flash with something before returning to their normal stare of hatred that I've witnessed since walking in.

"I didn't know what else to do, Kyle." My voice is thick, it's the first time I've ever talked about that day... at least in this way. People know about Lou, and they know I left... but aside from Dr. Tinnin, no one really knows. I'm expecting him to understand, I don't know why, but I just feel like he should understand what I'm saying. Be able to see the pain on my face while I'm explaining everything to him.

"Get out." The words fall so easily from his mouth that I'm not sure I've heard him correctly. "Get the fuck out." He turns, not letting me say anything else before he walks past where he was working when I came in and ducks through a door toward the back. I sigh, feeling my shoulders slump before turning toward the entrance and stepping back outside.

I guess this isn't going to be as easy to fix as I had hoped it would.

11

LOU

IT'S BEEN a week since I ran into Declan at Kyle's bar. One long fucking week of torturing myself with memories of him. Memories that no matter how hard I fucking try, keep flooding my mind. My emotions have been all over the place ever since, and everyone I work with is probably sick and tired of me.

I'm heading to my parents' house for family dinner night, and one thing I can always count on is my niece and nephew to cheer me up. And for the first time all week, as soon as I open my car door and hear them screaming my name from the side of my parents house, a smile fills my face.

"Hi, guys!" I shout back, shutting my door and jogging in their direction. They wrap their tiny arms around me and I bear hug them back. "I missed you."

"More!" they both shout. At least that's what I think they say, but who knows with two year old vocabulary.

"No way, José." I reach down and tickle them both.

They laugh at my rhyme before grabbing my hand and walking me into the backyard of my parents' home.

It's one of my favorite places to be, it's large and open with a huge covered patio. A lit outdoor fireplace sits off in the corner, it still isn't too cold outside, but just enough to make you want to go in after an hour. I look around the patio and sigh, it was one of my favorite places to study when I'd come home for the weekend from college.

Of course now, their large lot of green grass is occupied by a trampoline and jungle gym. Because their grandkids couldn't just have a swing set, they needed the best of the best.

When my parents found out Kyle was going to be a father, they were over the moon. They never once questioned Tessa and welcomed her with open arms. I've watched my parents fall head over heels in love with their grandchildren.

Once we get closer to the patio, Lane and Lucy take off in the direction of the jungle gym. Their giggles are the only sound in the backyard as they play together. Which is usually short lived because they can't agree on anything for long.

"Ah, to be a child." My mom sits on the large outdoor sectional, her feet propped on the coffee table in front of her, crossed at the ankles. She has a glass of wine in her hands, sipping as she stares out at the kids.

"They sure have energy." I laugh, stepping closer to her. I hug her before making my way inside for my own glass of wine. Tessa has just poured herself a glass but passes it to me when I step through the door.

"Here." She smiles, pouring a second glass.

We both walk back outside to sit with mom. My

brother and dad come through the garage door a few minutes later, deep in discussion about who knows what. Kyle smacks me in the back of the head, so in true sister fashion I nut check him. He coughs, and it brings a smile to my face while my mom shakes her head beside me.

"I swear, you two just never quit, do you," she says.

"He started it," I point out, her brows raise in question but she knows I'm right.

"Whatever." Kyle shakes his head. "You didn't have to hit me there."

"You didn't have to hit me at all, but yet here we are." I gesture with my arms around the patio.

He rolls his eyes, a smile playing on his lips despite what I just did to him and walks in the direction of the grill where our dad is.

"What are we having?" I lean against the soft, off-white cushions as I watch my dad open the grill.

"Chicken," my mom answers for him as she turns her head toward me. "And hotdogs of course." She chuckles, letting her eyes move past mine to her grandkids.

Her laugh grounds me. I love my mom, more than she will ever know.

"I'm starving," Tessa chimes in, rubbing a hand over her stomach.

"Same," I say. "I missed lunch today."

"Lou." My mom tilts her head at me, warning me.

"I know, I know." I wave her off. "I was just busy with patients."

When everything happened with Declan, I stopped eating. I didn't want to be alive, and felt like I was already dead. Looking back now, I realize how ridiculous I was for putting myself through what I did. I loved Declan with my whole heart, and the feelings are still there, but he was never worth ending my life.

I'm sure that Kyle has filled them in on him being back in town, and if I know my mother, I know that she is scared. When I say that time of my life was bad, I mean it was bad.

But, I'm not the same fragile girl I was fifteen years ago. I'm stronger, and it's going to take a hell of a lot more than seeing Declan in a bar to throw me off this time around.

"Have you talked to Peter?" Tessa asks, leaning her head against the cushion, but rolling it in my direction.

"Surprisingly, *no*. It's weird though, I thought he'd have a lot more to say but it's been crickets." I haven't talked to him since he moved out. Although, I haven't texted him. I've not had anything to say, and I guess he's enjoying wherever it is he's staying.

"That's good, at least. No drama."

"One-hundred percent." I laugh.

I'm not sure that I have the energy to fight with Peter and deal with my raging emotions from Declan being back.

"Dinner's ready," Dad shouts as he pulls the chicken from the grill and heads inside. Four little feet pound across the grass and through the back door, they rush down the hallway toward the bathroom where they wash up for dinner. Kyle follows behind him as the rest of us stand, following behind and doing the same.

My dad's food was amazing, not that I expected anything less. It's always amazing. Dinner was full of laughs, the kids had us rolling with them trying to say "weiner" in reference to their hotdogs. Which is probably inappropriate but look at who their dad is afterall.

The kids finish eating and are ready to keep playing, Tessa helps them get their coats on and they shoot straight out the backdoor to play again. She stands next to the glass door, watching them quietly.

"Well," my dad says, looking over at my mom. He reaches across the table and grabs her hand in his. "Your mother and I have something we want to discuss with you all."

"Oh, God. You're pregnant." Kyle covers his hands in a joking way, causing the entire table to giggle.

"At least Lou could be your doctor," Tessa adds from where she stands.

I'm just staring at my brother and silently cursing him for putting that image in my head.

"Don't I wish." Dad wiggles his brows, and my brother gags.

Serves him right.

"Oh, God. Make it stop." He rubs at his eyes frantically, trying to wash that image that was in my head and is now in his out.

"Your mother and I would like to renew our vows to one another. It's been nearly thirty-six years of marriage, and we want to recommit to each other." My dad smiles at my mom. "It's not every day that you get to spend your life with your best friend, and I'm so thankful that I have this chance."

"Aww." Tessa swoons at my dad's words, and I have to say, I do too.

My dad was the best role model for what a man should

be for a woman when I was growing up, and I honestly thought I had found that in Declan.

"When were you thinking?" I look at my parents, waiting for the answer.

"Well, we're not sure yet. We do know we want to have it here, in the home we built," my mom answers, she looks over her shoulder out the backdoor. Behind the kids playset is a large open lot of beautiful green grass that would be perfect for a small vow renewal ceremony.

"I think that's a great idea," I tell them.

I can picture it all in my head, small and intimate which is right up my parents' alley.

"Well, we'll keep you all updated on our plans."

After a little more talk, they all head back out to watch the kids while I decide it's time for me to call it a night. I'm exhausted from the day and just want to be in my bed.

After saying goodbye to everyone, and prying a sad faced Lucy from my leg with promises of a park trip tomorrow, I'm finally heading home. When I walk in, it's dark and reminds me of how lonely this place can be. I should have brought the kids home with me, but I'm just so tired tonight and my energy is running out.

I shower quickly before climbing into bed and pulling my laptop to sit on my lap. For a few minutes, I scroll through Facebook and see Tim's profile pop up. He added me after our talk in the park when I had the kids with me. I accepted because I meant what I said about letting the past be the past.

But I'm kind of regretting it right now because a picture of him and Declan from the bar the other night is filling my screen. His arm is thrown around Declan's shoulder as they smile at the camera.

Declan has that type of smile that makes everyone around him smile. You can't help it, it's a gift he has. His brown hair looks like it's had a few hands run through it, and I immediately wonder who he was with that night before I swallow the jealousy and remind myself that he's not mine. Not anymore.

Clicking off, I open my email to see if I've gotten anything new on my personal account lately. I forget to check it, I'm always more focused on my work email that I neglect my personal account. Granted, it's usually only for business newsletters so I can keep track of any sales happening at my favorite stores.

I have only one actual email that isn't trying to get me to buy anything that's twenty percent off. It's from my nemesis, and I roll my eyes as soon as I see her name but click on it anyways.

Hi Everyone!!!
   I can't believe it's time for our fifteen year reunion.
   I've attached the details below and can't wait to see everyone.
   Love always,
   Jillian

I ROLL my eyes at the screen. I've purposely avoided Jillian since the day I walked out of the gym after our high school graduation. She was always the super popular girl in school, the one with the bright blonde hair and the pretty smile. But she was catty as hell underneath all that makeup she wore and I never understood why more people didn't see it.

We never got along in school and she always had a crush on Declan. Even going as far as to ask him to take her home from school every day until I finally snapped. Who asks someone else's boyfriend to take them home every single day?

Jealousy isn't really my most glamorous moment from school, but I didn't like any girls messing with my man.

My man. I used to repeat that to him all the time, letting him know that I was his and he was mine. The laptop alerts that I've received a text, so instead of getting up to look for my phone, I respond on the screen of my MacBook.

Nicole: Bitch! This reunion.

Me: I know.

I add an eye roll so she can get the full effect of my annoyance of what I've just read.

Nicole: Are you going to go? I think Roger and I are. It's free food and free drinks.

Me: I don't know...

It's not that I don't want to go... okay, it's totally that I don't want to go. I've avoided a lot of people since high school, and I don't really want to spend an evening listening to them talk about their fake, happy lives and how much better off they are than me. And I know that's exactly what Jillian will do once she sees me. It won't matter the success I've had, because I'm single and I don't have any kids.

She'll use it against me, even though she's had plenty of failed relationships and doesn't have kids either. Somehow, she'll make my situation seem far worse than her own.

Nicole: You have to come with us. It'll be fun.

Me: Nic! Why on earth do you want to go?

Nicole: I told you, free food, free drinks. It's a win, win. Plus, I want to give Jillian a hard time.

Me: Easy for you to say.

Nicole: Oh, c'mon. You're a fucking babe, always have been always will be. You're going to go shopping with me, buy a new dress that highlights that perfectly toned ass of yours and you're going to flaunt it in front of her face.

I let what she's said resonate in me. She's right, I've got to stop letting Jillian get under my skin. Hell, it's been fifteen years and I haven't been to a single reunion yet. Jillian tries to plan them for every five years but half the class doesn't bother to attend.

Me: Well, when you put it like that...

Nicole: YES!!! You can ride with us. Let's plan something for shopping.

For the next ten minutes, Nicole and I talk about plans and where we'd like to shop for our dresses. By the time I close my eyes, sleep consumes me faster than it has all week.

12

DECLAN

I SPENT the morning with my mom. We had lunch at her favorite diner that just opened about a year ago. She told me all about it while we ate, and the food wasn't that bad. It's probably somewhere I'll eat from time to time, while I'm here, that is. However long that's going to be. It's still undecided and in the hands of Dr. Tinnin.

Part of me wants to put my roots down here, call this place home again. It holds a lot of good memories for me, but there's still that one memory that hurts more than anything. And because of that, I'm not sure if I can stay here.

For now, I'm enjoying this time with my mom. Which is why we're taking a walk around town. Her arm is linked in mind as we cross the street, heading toward the downtown area.

Fall weather has moved in, which means they have a fall festival they're preparing for. It's one of the biggest events of the year here, and my mom is on the council that plans it all. A small courtyard sits in the center of the town square, directly across from the courthouse. Many members are unpacking boxes of decorations, some that have been around since I was a kid.

I remember the first time Lou and I came to the festival together. Man, she was the prettiest girl and she was on my arm all night. I felt like a Goddamn king.

"You excited for the festival?" she asks, her eyes locked on what we're walking toward.

"I don't know if I'll go," I tell her, shrugging my shoulders.

"Declan Sanchez, you *will* be going." She releases my arm. "Besides, I have plenty of work you can do for it to keep you busy."

I shake my head, knowing there's no use in arguing with her and let a small smile show.

"Whatever you say, Momma."

"If only getting you to agree to something else was that easy."

I sigh as she says it, already knowing what she's refer-ring to.

She wants me out of the military, *for good*. She hated that I joined in the first place and doesn't understand why I feel the need to continue my service.

It's the one and only thing my mother and I argue about. Almost every time we talk.

She wanted my dad out, but he refused to leave. Said it was who he was when he met her, and it's who he'd be when he left her. Little did he know, he meant those words in a different way.

When he died, it gutted her. I watched my mom lose herself, everyday. I was the one taking care of her, and I never dealt with my father's death the way I was supposed to and never bothered with therapy for it. Once I knew my mom was going to be okay and Aunt B would be here for her, I left to join.

Something told me it was the right thing to do, that it was my dad's legacy and I needed to follow through with it myself. Joining made me feel closer to him than I ever did while he was here. He was a fucking great dad, he was just always gone because he was deployed. I knew I wouldn't be able to leave if I had Lou with me, and after watching my mom all my life when he was gone and how she was when he passed, I knew I had to end things.

To keep her safe and to protect her heart.

"Mom." I'm stern, needing her to understand. "We've talked about this, I'm not leaving the military until my time is up."

"Your time is up soon, son. You don't have to re-enlist, I don't know why you're doing this. You're all I have left in this world, and you're willing to take the last thing I have from me?"

Her words gut me as I watch the tears in her eyes form. It's not unusual for my mom to guilt trip me with this topic.

"Momma." My voice softens but she takes a step back when I reach for her.

"I'm going to go home, I need to call your aunt." She starts to turn, but I grab her elbow and gently spin her to face me.

"Mom, please don't be mad." I look at her, trying to gauge her reaction.

"Oh, boy." Her hand slides up to rest on my cheek. "I'm not mad, I'm hurt." Her hand falls and she turns, walking in the opposite direction of where we just came from, the direction that would take her home.

My chest is heavy, full of pain and guilt for my decisions. Even though I don't feel like I'm doing anything wrong. I don't know how to win in this situation.

I run a hand through my hair and look around me. This entire fucking town hurts to even look at. There's not a single memory here that doesn't flood back when I walk through it.

Hurting my mom was never what I wanted, I just didn't know any other way to feel my dad again and I desperately needed that. I didn't join to hurt her, or to hurt Lou. I did it for my own selfish reasons, then it became something I loved. Feeling important and like I was making a part in history, protecting people. It's what I wanted, and it was easier to do it since I didn't have Lou.

After walking around the square and greeting everyone on the council, I head down a side street that walks you past the park. Children's laughter fills the air the closer I get, and I don't remember the park ever not sounding this happy. It's one of the best parts of this town.

The park was my dad's favorite part of the town. When he was home, he'd make it a point to take me every single day. It was something that was just ours. I shake my head, pushing down the pain those memories bring up, reminding me that he's not here anymore. The closer I get to the edge of the park, the more of the play area comes into view. My eyes always go straight to the swingset first. It was my favorite part of the entire area, we'd swing for nearly an hour every time.

I'd show him how high I could go before jumping out of the seat and landing on my feet. He'd laugh, tell me never to let my mom see that and ruffle my hair with his hand.

A dad pushes his son, the child giggles the higher the swing goes, begging his dad to push him higher and higher. He's small, maybe a couple years old and holding on tightly to the baby swing he's in.

I remember that feeling, being so carefree and thinking nothing could ever change.

The sight in front of me makes me miss my dad more. I grab at my chest, massaging away the ache from losing him. It doesn't matter how long it's been, it still fucking sucks and hurts just like yesterday.

More giggling causes me to turn my head, and when I do my jaw drops to the floor. She's the last person I expected to see, especially here.

A little girl with long blonde hair pulled into a ponytail runs up to her wrapping her arms around her legs. She bends, rubbing her hand along the girl's back.

My feet are moving before I even realize where they're carrying me. Straight to the girl that holds my heart in her hands. Lou looks up when she sees me approaching before looking back down at the little girl.

"Go play with your daddy for a second." My eyes flicker to the little girl before moving back to the ocean blue ones staring at me. I see red for a moment, hearing that she has a kid, and with someone else. I knew this could happen.

No, that it would happen, but it stings all the same. I'm feeling something sinister inside me, because some other man has had what's mine. What's always been mine, even though I have no right to feel the way I do right now.

13

LOU

EMERALD GREEN EYES glare into mine as he approaches. He's the last person I expected to see here today. Lucy pulls on my hand, and I slowly tear my eyes from Declan and look at her.

"An Wew." Her voice is so soft. "Swide me?"

I nod, looking back up at Declan to see his shoulders relax.

"Go play with your daddy for a second."

Lucy looks in the direction of where my eyes are focused before she runs off in the direction of Kyle and Lane.

I wrap my arms around myself, pretending it's from the chill in the air today and not because the man walking toward me makes me nervous. The look in his eyes makes my stomach drop, straight to my toes. It's intense and I hate that he looks sexy as hell while he walks toward me.

Those eyes still bring chillbumps to my skin and takes everything I have in me to pull mine away from his.

His jeans hang low on his slim hips, and for some reason,

all I want to do is reach out and touch him. He was always in shape, but never like this. He's wearing a solid black t-shirt with a flannel lined jacket covering it. Even with his torso hidden, I can still tell that there is stone under his clothes. He works out, probably more than I ever have in my lifetime.

"Lou." He says my name with a voice so deep and low, that it brings a shiver to my spine. It's different from that night in the bar, and I don't know why. Maybe because I know he's in town now and I didn't know he'd be there that night.

My eyes dart to where Kyle is playing with the kids, he's completely preoccupied by Lane on the swing and Lucy is now situated in the one next to them.

"It's nice to see you again." He looks me in the eyes and it makes me feel so small.

I tuck a piece of hair behind my ear, a nervous habit of mine. His lip lifts in a smirk, and that single movement brings back so many memories. Declan was always cocky, but in a way that isn't annoying.

"What are you doing here?" I lift my eyes to him as I ask the question I've been dying to hear the answer to. There's a fire burning in those verdant eyes. One that I know all too well about.

"I was with my mom, just taking a walk." He looks over his shoulder in the direction he just came from. I'm guessing they were in the square since his mom helps with the town council for the fall festivities each year. "Where's Tim?"

My brows pinch together at his question. Why the fuck would he be asking about Tim? I flick my eyes back to Kyle and thankfully the kids still hold his attention.

"What?" I look back at him, still confused why he'd be asking me about Tim Schaeder of all people.

"Tim? Your boyfriend?"

Oh, shit. A small smile appears on his lips.

When I said that I didn't realize it would come back to bite me in the ass. Hell, I sure didn't think about the fact that I'd be running into him again. The longer I take to answer, the larger his smile grows. He fucking knows I'm lying about Tim.

"He's, uh," I pause, trying to think of an excuse, "he had to work today." That's pretty solid, right?

"Work, huh?"

I nod, answering his question.

"Where's he work?"

Ah, shit. Where does Tim work? Fuck, I don't even know.

Thankfully, I don't have to answer because a loud giggle catches his attention. His head slowly turns to where the kids are playing. "She's cute, looks a lot like you." He's referring to Lucy. "I can't believe you're a mom," he says, shaking his head.

"Oh," My brows shoot up and I shake my head with a smile. "She's not mine." His eyes snap back to mine, and I swear his shoulders drop an inch. "She's Kyle's." I point to my brother. "And that's his son."

"Kyle's?" he asks, almost as if he can't believe it.

Trust me bud, we couldn't believe it either.

"Wow. Twins?" He looks back at me, shoving his hands in the pockets of his jacket.

"Yeah. They're two." I smile at them, they really do bring me so much happiness.

"So, uh," he pauses. "Can we get together some time? Catch up?"

I'm about to tell him that I don't think that's a good idea, but I'm suddenly pushed back a step and my brother is standing in front of me. Lucy and Lane are a few feet away, confused by this side of their dad. I don't hear what Kyle is saying because I'm walking toward the kids and dropping down in front of them.

"You two go play, and maybe we can stop by the bakery on the way home." Their eyes light up and the situation with their dad is forgotten as they run as hard as they can to play.

"I told you to stay the fuck away from her." Kyle's in his face, but Declan doesn't move.

I move back to where I was standing, trying to separate the two of them. "We're in a park full of kids, guys."

"I just wanted to talk to her, explain some things." Declan doesn't look down at me, his eyes are fixed on Kyle.

"She doesn't need your explanations. She's been fine without you for fifteen years, Declan." My brother takes a step toward Declan, but when I push on his chest he moves back to where he was.

"I didn't want any problems, I just wanted to talk," Declan says to me this time.

I nod in understanding. Declan takes a small step in my direction but Kyle is pushing him backwards, his forehead nearly pressing into Declan's and I'm pushed out of the way.

Stepping between the two of them again, I press a hand to Kyle's chest before doing the same to Declan. I wish I could say that the touch doesn't phase me, but it does. The feel of his solid chest under the palm of my hand burns against my skin. Declan notices because his eyes drop to my hand before moving back to my eyes and I see the pain that floats through his eyes.

I feel it, too.

Declan sighs, looking at Kyle before slowly moving his eyes back to mine. He shakes his head, before taking a step back, turning on his heels and leaving the park. Kyle pushes my hand from his chest and turns his back to me, with his hands rested on the back of his head.

"Kyle," I start. "You can't fucking react like that every-time he's around. We're in a damn park, with *your* kids." He turns then, eyes wide as he glances over at them. "They're fine, I told them you'd take them to the bakery."

"Shit." He runs a hand over his face. "I lost it."

"Yeah, you did." I look back at Declan, watching as he walks down the sidewalk. Right before he disappears, he looks over his shoulder and those green eyes pierce me.

"Are you okay?" Kyle grabs my arm, pulling me in for a hug. "I'm sorry."

I don't answer him, he holds my head against his chest and I let him hold me for a minute as I think about the past and how we ended up where we are today.

And how after all these years, that man still has such a hold over my heart.

———

A FEW HOURS LATER, I'm in the front seat of Nicole's car and heading toward a boutique. They sell a little bit of everything, from maternity to fancy dinner dresses.

"Declan showed up at the park this morning." I break the silence in the car.

"Holy shit. Wasn't Kyle with you?"

I nod.

"How'd he handle that?" She looks over, but averts her eyes back to the road just as quickly.

"Oh, he was pissed." I chuckle. "He was in his face and I had to bribe the kids with the bakery so they didn't see or hear what was being said."

"Damn." Her head shakes slightly. "What'd he want?"

"He wanted to talk. Something about catching up so he could explain." I shrug my shoulders. "But honestly, I don't need an explanation. Not anymore. That was so long ago, I don't even care what his reason could be. It means nothing at this point."

As much as I want my words to be true, I know they aren't. I feel like part of me needs to know why he did what he did all those years ago, but then another part of me wants to be a badass bitch that isn't affected by him anymore. Which is a lie.

It blows my mind that I still can't get over this man. A man who broke me when I thought I had the world in my hands. A man who promised to love me, only to leave me stranded with my heart in tiny fragments and a tear stained face.

"That is weird for him to all of a sudden want to explain why he was such a fuck up fifteen years ago." She hits her blinker, easing off the road and pulling alongside the curb.

"I don't know." I open the door, slinging my purse over my shoulder and wait for her to meet me on the sidewalk. "It's just odd, after all this time."

"Yeah." We fall in step beside each other and walk into the boutique. "You know what?"

I look over at her, hearing the door of the boutique chime. "What?"

"You're going to look fucking hot at the reunion, and show him exactly what his dumbass has been missing all these years." She smirks.

"Umm, no." I laugh. "Not a chance."

The sales woman approaches, explaining a few sales they have going on. "If you need anything, please let me know."

"Thank you," Nicole tells her, turning her attention back to me. "And why not?"

"Because, I don't want him to think I'm trying to do anything where he's involved."

"You're a way better woman than me, babe." She shakes her head. "Way better."

Nicole walks in the direction of the back of the store, flipping through a few racks as she goes while I start looking for myself. The first rack I come to, my hand connects with a little black dress that is my size. I pull it from the rack and examine it closer. It's classy, and not at all revealing so Nicole probably wouldn't approve of it for what she wanted the reunion to be.

"That's pretty." Her voice startles me, causing me to bump into the rack.

"Damn you."

She laughs. "Buy it." She winks, turning and heading toward the jewelry. I look back down at the dress and make the decision to try it on.

The saleswoman gets me situated in the dressing room,

and when I step out to look at myself in the mirror I hear Nicole.

"Holy. Fucking. Shit." I look over at her, her mouth is hanging open with a hint of a smile hidden. "That dress was made for you."

"I agree." The sales woman nods.

Turning my attention back to the dress, I smile at myself.

Is it wrong to make him regret his decision to leave? Probably, but I'd be lying if I said I wasn't honestly tempted to try.

14

DECLAN

"Why are you doing this? What did I do wrong?" The tears pool in her eyes, and I can feel my heart shattering as I watch her.

I hate this. I don't want to do it, but I don't know any other way. I need to get out of here, out of this fucking town. Everywhere I look, I see my dad and when I'm not being reminded of him I'm watching my mom struggle to cope with being a widow.

Joining the military is my only chance. The only way I know how to feel close to him again, the only downfall is leaving her behind.

But I can't ask her to go. I'll never ask her to leave her family or watch her become my mother when I'm gone. Always on edge each time the phone rings, thinking it'll be that dreaded call or fearing that the door bell will ring and it'll all be over.

"Talk to me. It's the least you could do." Her composure snaps, and for a moment I pause and rethink everything. "Is this about your dad? Just talk to me, we can work this out. Please!" she begs.

Something wet slides across my jaw, causing my eyes to pop open. The only thing I see is a giant snout and two beedy eyes staring at me. When I don't move immediately,

Gunnar let's his tongue slide across my face again. This time from my chin to my forehead. His wagging tail shakes the entire bed, and even if I wanted to go back to sleep, he wouldn't let me.

Not that I want to return to that dream anyways. It's always the same. I'm plagued by the look on her face that day when I walked away. When I made the hardest decision I have ever made. One I regret daily.

My eyes scan my childhood bedroom, nothing's changed. A small maple desk sits off in the corner of the room, the same pens and pencils in the coffee cup with the Army logo displayed on the front. Above it are pictures from my childhood, several with Kyle when things weren't so bitter between us.

Even though I don't blame him for the way he's treated me since I've been back in town. I deserve it and would do the same thing in his situation.

The one that always makes my heart ache though, is the one of Lou. We were at the park and the wind was blowing her hair as she sat on the swingset. I begged her for the picture, because she was just fucking perfect that day. I remember staring at her and feeling the ache in my chest because I loved her so much then.

And still do.

The smell of bacon wakes my senses and I'm on my feet and heading down the hallway in the next instance, leaving behind the painful memories of my past.

My mom stands in front of the stove, flipping the bacon before cracking a few eggs into a separate pan.

"Good morning." Mom turns, letting her eyes slide to mind before she turns back to her cooking.

Great. She's still pissed.

"Can we talk about yesterday?" I step into the room, heading for the coffee maker and pour myself a cup.

I watch as she forks the bacon onto a plate, and scoops an egg onto the plate before handing it to me.

"Thank you," I tell her, turning toward the table and wait for her to join me.

"Listen," she sighs, making her own plate and sits beside me, "I know you've made a career of the military, and I'm so proud of you for it." She shakes her head. "God bless everyone that does, but dammit, why does it have to be you, Declan?"

My mother never cusses, so thank God I haven't taken a bite yet or I probably would have choked on my food.

I groan. "Mo–"

"Why you? You've been gone long enough, why do you feel the need to serve more? You're all I have left in this world, sweet boy." A tear falls and I have to look away. "Look at me." She reaches out, pulling my chin so that I have no choice but to look at her. "I lost your father far too early. We had many years left together, and he was taken too soon. I can't lose you, my boy. I won't survive it again."

"Mom, it's my life now. I need you to understand."

"Need me to understand?" she scoffs. "What? That you feel you have to continue this in order to feel closer to him?"

I lean back, not expecting to hear those words.

"You can feel close to him in a million different ways, Declan, not just putting your life on the line constantly. You've served your country, now it's time to come home. Look at everything you've given up."

She's referring to Lou, and I look away again, refusing to let her see the emotion that bubbles to the surface at the mention of her name. What a fucked up day this is going to be. First with my dream of her, now this.

"Just please consider it." Her eyes plead with mine when I look back at her.

"I will." And it's the truth.

She smiles, grabbing the salt before sliding it across the table to me. "Now, tell me about this run in that you had with Kyle."

"Word travels fast, huh?" I laugh, taking a bite of bacon. "It was nothing."

"Sure." She smirks, side-eying me as she starts in on her own plate.

"He just doesn't want me around Lou," I admit.

"He is protective of her, I'll give him that. Her last boyfriend wasn't the best from what I've heard," she tells me.

The thought of Lou being with someone else still causes my blood to boil, but I don't have any right to be mad. My mom starts laughing, pulling me from my thoughts.

"What?"

"The look on your face." She smiles. "It tells me all I need to know."

I shake my head, focusing back on my breakfast.

———

"DECLAN, HOW ARE YOU TODAY?" Dr. Tinnin asks through the small screen of my laptop.

"I'm good, how are you?" I smile.

"You're smiling, I'm assuming you've been having better days?" he asks.

"Not exactly." I laugh, running my hand through my hair.

"And why is that?"

"Well, I ran into Lou," I explain.

"Again?"

I nod. "Yeah, this time it was at the park. She was with her brother."

"How was that interaction?"

"Not the best. Her brother and I nearly fought once, and again at the park," I tell him. I think back to the look in Lou's eyes.

"Oh? Fighting isn't the answer, Declan, I'm sure you know that." He smiles at me.

"I do, I asked her if we could get together to catch up."

"Good, I think that's a great idea. A good way for you to express your feelings about everything that has gone on. What'd she say?" he asks, writing something down while waiting for me to answer.

"She didn't. That was when her brother got involved."

"I see," he mutters. "What else has been going on?"

"We have a fifteen year school reunion. I got an email the other day about it." I hadn't even known they were doing reunions anymore, not until I randomly checked my email after I'd stalked Lou on facebook for an hour.

Which was a mistake, all I did was find picture after picture of her and I'm assuming her ex boyfriend. What I didn't find though, were any pictures of her and Tim.

"Are you going to go?"

"Yeah, I think so. I don't necessarily want to, but I'm hoping Lou will be there."

We spend the rest of the session talking about the

reunion, what I expect will come from it and everything that's been going on with my mom.

He reminded me that my mom's feelings and fear are justified, but at the end of the day, it's my life that I have to make the decision for. He ended the session by telling me he was impressed with the progress that seems to be occurring since I returned home.

For the first time ever, I didn't feel defeated or pissed off by the end of our talk. I felt like I was heading in the right direction, I just didn't know what direction that was.

15

LOU

I'VE BEEN DREADING this reunion all week. I shouldn't have agreed to go, I would have been just as happy staying home and doing absolutely nothing for the night.

It's a bad idea... I can feel it.

Of course Nicole wouldn't let me stay home.

The only thing that will get me through the rest of this day is knowing that it's Friday, I only have half a work day left, and Kyle and I are having lunch in a little bit.

I knock on one of the exam rooms before pushing inside. "Hello."

"Hello, Dr. Tucker," Cecily responds.

Cecily is young, barely eighteen and pregnant with her first child. She's planning on attending the local community college and I've been doing all that I can to make sure that she has every possible resource available to her. She's essentially alone, her parent's haven't spoken to her since they found out she was pregnant and that's put Cecily through a lot of stress.

"How's everything going?" I smile, turning to wash my hands.

"It's going good." She smiles back at me.

"Good." I dry my hands and turn to face her. "Today we're just going to do a quick ultrasound and then send you off for some blood work."

"Okay." She anxiously bites her bottom lip but lays back on the exam table, allowing me to get started. "I hate needles."

"I completely understand." I giggle, walking over to the ultrasound machine.

I go through everything, showing her the baby and explain that everything looks to be right on track. Once I'm finished, I say my goodbyes and leave the room.

"Your brother's waiting for you in your office." Talia walks past me in the hall, heading for the break room with her empty coffee mug.

"Thanks." I drop the iPad off at the nurses station and walk toward my office. Talia walks back down the hall towards the receptionist area. "I'll be leaving shortly for lunch, if there are any problems let me know."

"You got it." She smiles and pushes through the door.

My office door is open when I reach it, with Kyle sitting in a chair across from my desk with his phone in his hand.

"Are you sexting your wife?" I laugh.

"Always." He stands, shoving his phone in his pocket.

I make a fake gagging sound... because gross.

"You ready?" he asks, standing and taking a step closer to the door. "I'm fucking starving."

"Yeah." I grab my coat from behind the door, pushing

my arms through before grabbing my phone and purse and shutting the door behind us.

Kyle drives to the restaurant, which is just on the other side of town. He pulls into the first available spot before climbing out, so I do the same. We're silent until we're seated.

"I can't believe Mom and Dad are renewing their vows." He grabs a chip from the bowl in the center of the table and dips it into the salsa, letting it drop across the table before taking a bite.

"You're the nastiest person I know." I scrunch my nose at him. "I don't know how Tessa puts up with you." I'm surprised she hasn't hired a cleaning service to come in and follow Kyle around the house, as messy as he is.

"Me either, honestly." He shrugs. "I'm just a lucky son of a bitch."

"That you are," I agree with him.

Dread builds inside me. My stomach drops when the thought hits me that I may never have what they have.

"Why can't you believe Mom and Dad are renewing their vows?" I say, changing the subject.

"I don't know, it seems weird to me." he looks at me and shrugs his shoulders before popping another chip in his mouth.

"Probably because you married the first girl you ever dated." I laugh, and a chip is thrown at me.

"Shut up." He rolls his eyes, taking another chip and doing the same as before. Dripping the salsa across the table.

I slide a napkin across to him, but he doesn't take it so I end up wiping the mess up myself. "You're seriously so gross."

"Meh." He crunches a chip in his mouth, smiling in the process.

The waitress comes, taking our order before disappearing again.

"So, have you heard anymore from Declan?" Kyle's mood changes as he asks. It's sad to see, knowing that the two of them used to be so close at one point.

"No, I haven't seen him since that day at the park."

"Good," he grunts. "I don't even know why he came home."

"Well, his mom lives here." I shrug, not sure how to answer him. My first instinct is to always defend him, and I don't even have a solid reason why I should. I just always do.

"So?" He snaps his eyes to mine. "She could go to him."

Hearing him talk this way hurts my feelings, which is ridiculous and makes me feel like an idiot for having these emotions for someone that treated me so badly in the past. Well, I wouldn't say *badly*, I mean the break up was shitty, but the rest of our relationship was damn near perfect. I just hate how everything turned out, for everyone.

Kyle notices my change in mood. "What's wrong?" He drops the chip in his hand, looking at me with concerned eyes.

"I feel so dumb." I flatten my lips, trying to avert my eyes to the ceiling to keep the tears at bay.

"What?" His eyes widen and he leans forward. "Why?"

"Because, after everything I still can't seem to fucking let go." I admit, and that was easier to say than I thought it would be. Like a little piece of the weight on my shoulders I've been carrying has slowly lifted. He doesn't say anything, but a deep frown forms on his face. "Like I still think about him every damn day and if anyone says anything bad," I trail off, tucking a strand of my hair behind my ear because I'm nervous of how he'll react. "I still have this need to defend him."

"Why?" he scoffs like it's the most ridiculous thing he's ever heard. And it just may be. "Why do you still feel this way, Lou? After everything he's done to you?"

"I don't know, Kyle. I don't know." I shake my head, trying to get my thoughts straight. "I still love him."

His eyes widen at my admission, and my heart is thundering against my ribcage as I watch all the emotions pass across my brother's face. He went from shock, to fear, to worry in about three seconds.

"He needs to leave town." Kyle grips the edge of the table, his knuckles turning white before he pushes away from the table, leaning against the back of his chair and turning his attention to the front door. "He shouldn't have come back, and you wouldn't be feeling like this."

"No, it's not just him returning. I've had a shitty few months," I point out, trying to make him understand that it isn't all Declan coming home. It's a major part of it, but it's not *all* of it. I've dealt with a breakup, feeling insecure and fearful of him being unfaithful, watching everyone around me have their happily ever afters, while I go home alone each night, and then there's Declan returning.

"Don't I know it," he snaps.

I jerk back, like a slap in the face. I feel the anger in his words.

"I'm sorry." He shakes his head. "I didn't mean it like that."

"Then how did you mean it?" I need him to clarify this one.

"Lou," his voice softens with my name, "I just meant that it's not fucking fair that you've had to deal with everything you've been going through. First with that asshole Peter and now this shit with Declan."

"Is it bad that I'm like this?" I dab at the corner of my eye, glancing around the restaurant to see if anyone is watching the show taking place.

"No, pain isn't easy to get over. I just don't want him to drag you back down," he admits.

"I know, and it won't. I won't let him."

"Yeah, but we don't know that, Lou."

I pause, my brother's feelings for Declan are clear and he hasn't been secretive about hiding them.

"I won't let him tear you down again. I know you've struggled with getting over him, but damn... It's been how long? Remember what he fucking did to you, Lou. Do you know how hard it was to see you that way?"

"You know what?" I stand, placing my napkin on the table. I need out of here before I break. No one has to remind me what it was like when he left me, I remember it all very vividly like it was yesterday. "I think I'm going to go."

"Lou, stop. I'm sorry. I didn't mean to lose my cool."

"No, I'm going to call Nicole to come get me. I'll see you next week." I look at him.

"Lou, please." He stands, drawing attention to us. "Don't go."

"I just want to be alone right now, okay?" I step around the table to him, leaning in and kissing him on the cheek. "I love you, but I can't sit here any longer and listen to this. I know he fucked me over, Kyle. I think about it every goddamn day, but I don't need you reminding me how hard it was for *you.*"

I don't say anything else, a quick glance around tells me that no one gives a shit about the spectacle that just took place so I turn and walk out of the restaurant, sending a quick text to Nicole to come pick me up.

My emotions are everywhere, and I'm not sure I can even go back to work today after that.

"Hello?" Talia answers on the first ring.

"Hey, I'm going to need to take the rest of the day off. Will you call all my clients and offer for them to see the nurse practitioner today or reschedule to see me next week sometime?" I explain, I feel shitty doing this but I'm not at my best to be treating anyone else today.

"Sure, is everything okay?" she asks, the concern in her voice makes my heart swell.

"Everything is fine," I lie.

Nothing has been fine for a while.

WHEN I WOKE up this morning, I was flooded with the events of yesterday. Leaving my brother in the middle of the restaurant, upset and having to take the rest of the day off. When Nicole dropped me off, I sat in my living room with a giant tub of ice cream and wallowed in my emotions until I fell asleep.

I'll be lucky if this damn dress fits me after the junk food I devoured. But, it doesn't matter because I'm not trying to impress anyone. Right?

Fucking wrong. Regardless of everything, I still want to

make him want me. Make him see what he gave up. It's petty and selfish but do I care? No.

Now I'm standing in my foyer, waiting for Nicole to arrive with her husband, Roger, so I can third wheel it to the reunion with them. That's what my life has become, a third wheel.

Everywhere I go.

If I'm with my parents, I'm the third wheel. If I'm with Nicole and her husband, I'm the third wheel. If I'm with Kyle and Tessa, third fucking wheel.

And I'm sick of it.

I look in the mirror hanging just behind the door. I dab at my lips and run my fingers through my long hair to untangle some of the curls. Dread pools in my tummy at the thought of seeing Declan and being with all the catty bitches from high school again.

Ugh, Jillian especially.

The sound of my doorbell makes me jump, then laugh because I'm so caught up in my head that even a sound I've been waiting on startles me. When I pull it open, I see Nicole and her husband. Roger smiles, leaning in to place a kiss on my cheek.

"You look nice, Lou." He smiles at me.

"No," Nicole says, causing me to frown at her. "You look fucking *hot*." She fans herself before turning her attention to her husband. "Don't downplay her beauty." she scoffs and pushes him aside, lifting a bottle of whiskey in her hand. "I figured you'd need the hard shit."

"You have no idea." I smile, and head toward my kitchen for three shot glasses.

Thank God for a friend like Nicole who knows exactly what I need before I even realize what it is. She knew today would be hell for me, and even though she pushed me to attend, she's also taking care of me too.

"You okay?" she asks, coming up behind me.

"Yeah, I'm fine." I bite at my bottom lip, nervously, while trying to act like it's just another day. "I'll be even better once this is all over with though."

"Amen," Roger says, pulling a bar stool out and taking a seat on the edge. "I fucking hate class reunions."

Same. Which is why I've never been to any of ours until now, and to be honest, I don't give a damn about seeing anyone that we went to school with that often.

"Oh, hush. You've never even been to one." Nicole swats at him.

"Exactly, because I hate fucking reunions." He stares at her as if it should be obvious before she laughs and he pulls her between his legs. I watch the two of them and envy grows in my chest.

I want that. Someone to share that witty banter with.

I pour the whiskey over three shot glasses and slide one to each of them before lifting my own in my hand.

"He's going to regret coming back home." Nicole raises her glass. "To the fucking past." She clinks her glass against ours and tips it back.

It's not exactly the toast I would have given but since she's already downed hers and Roger is doing the same, I can't really toast for anything else... so, to the fucking past it is.

16

LOU

I was silent the entire way to the reunion. After about five minutes, both Roger and Nicole realized I wasn't going to be much for conversation on the way over and stopped talking to me.

This was a bad idea, I can feel it. I shouldn't have let her talk me into this.

The car slows as Roger pulls into the gym parking lot where the reunion is being held. Our old high school still looks exactly the same, except now a giant banner is hung from the outside welcoming students from our graduating class.

Roger and Nicole climb out once the car is parked, but I stay seated for a moment, trying to regain my composure. I'll have to put my game face on because one person I know waiting on me inside will try to slither under my skin like the snake she is.

Jillian Baker.

I couldn't stand her in high school, and I sure as hell can't stand her now. We see each other from time to time, but if I can help it I go out of my way to avoid her at all costs. She's a jealous, spiteful bitch who's hated me for as long as I can remember.

She carefully chooses her words so that she can form a rise out of me while also remaining sweet and innocent to everyone else.

How she was popular in school is beyond me. But so is her organizing this entire event, so there's that.

When the car parks, I release a breath I didn't realize I was holding. When I grab the handle, I pause, trying to muster up the courage to do this. Have you ever felt like something was such a bad idea? That you should just not go because it's going to be a disaster? That's how I'm feeling right now. My stomach is in knots and I feel like I could throw up at any moment.

I climb out of the car, placing a hand to my stomach to keep the nerves at bay. The last thing I need is for her to smell my fear when I walk inside, she'll eat that shit up like candy.

"You good?" Nicole asks, linking her arm with her husband's.

"Yeah." I straighten, pulling my dress down in place and lifting my boobs slightly so they're more perky. "Let's go."

"That's my girl." Nicole winks and takes the first step toward the building.

I hold my head high, smiling as we pass people we knew in school. Some that we haven't seen in years. A few stop and talk to us, one stands a little closer than I'd like, but I don't read too much into it. Jerry Reynolds was always nice in school, but never on my radar. Granted, I only had eyes for one guy back then.

He's changed a lot though, he's not the quiet, nerdy boy

who sat alone at lunch reading his science book. Now he's a man, with a nice smile. And if my heart wasn't still in shambles over Declan and the disaster that Peter caused, I'd probably be interested in him.

The air in the room changes, and I feel the hair on the back of my neck stand at attention.

He's here.

Turning, I catch sight of Declan as he steps through the front entrance. He's dressed in black slacks and a gray button down. The top few buttons are left open, and I swallow at the thought of what he looks like underneath the thin fabric. His blazer hugs his biceps like a glove, and I lick my lips at the sight of him.

Nicole elbows me in the side, and it's then that I realize Declan's eyes are locked on mine. His deep ocean colored eyes bore into mine before slowly moving down my body. I shift, feeling insecure as he devours me with that look.

And what do I do in response?

I laugh like a hyena, grabbing Jerry's arm and pretending to be interested in the conversation taking place. He doesn't seem phased by my outburst and I'm thankful for it.

This seems to be becoming a normal thing, where I just act a fool and do things without thinking when it comes to Declan.

I have no idea what I'm doing, but yet here I am trying to make Declan think he doesn't have a hold over me and doesn't affect me at all. When I glance back in Declan's direction, his eyes have moved from my to where my hand is still resting on Jerry's arm. His jaw ticks before his eyes bounce back to mine, a small smirk forming before he heads in our direction.

With each step he takes, I feel heat form in my chest at the sight of him. I think he's about to say something about me and Jerry, but when he approaches the small group we've formed, he ignores me completely.

"Jerry Reynolds." Declan holds a hand out. "How have you been, man?"

Jerry moves his arm, which just so happens to be the one my hand was on and shakes Declan's hand. I fight myself not to roll my eyes at the ridiculousness of this entire situation, knowing Declan only came over to say hi because I poked the damn beast.

Declan is a jealous man, or at least he was back in school. I can't really judge him on that now, but something about the smile he's wearing and the looks he keeps shooting my way as they conversate about the past tells me not much has changed.

"Nicole, beautiful as ever." Declan smiles down at her.

She thanks him, her eyes darting to mine for a brief moment before she introduces him to Roger.

I've had enough, already.

"I'm going to go find our table." I excuse myself and head into the main gym area, needing the escape.

A table is set up, just as you step inside the door with a pamphlet of our senior composite photos and a run down of the night's events. I stare at my image, remembering how happy I was back then. The girl smiling in that photo thought she had it all, little did she know she was going to feel empty all these years later.

That she'd jump all in with a man that never really deserved her or wanted her, but she didn't care because she was so heartbroken over the one man she wanted more than life.

I stare at Declan's picture, his eyes are bright, matching my own enthusiasm. My heart aches for those times, and what I would give to feel that type of happiness again... even if it was just for a little while.

"Here you go." I freeze, pamphlet in hand and cringe at the sound of that voice, the one person I could have really done without seeing today but knew it was inevitable.

Jillian smiles as she hands me my name tag.

"It is still Lou *Tucker*... right?" She smirks. Her insult climbing my skin just like she wanted. I feel my face heat at her words, but offer a small smile and take the name tag. "Here, let me."

I grit my teeth as she rounds the table, stepping into my bubble and attaching the name tag over my heart.

"It must be awful to be single at thirty-three." She chuckles.

I refrain from being catty and pulling her hair like I desperately want to. But, I am petty enough to point out that she's in the same fucking boat as I am. I'm about to remind her of that when her attention shifts from me to someone behind me.

"Oh, Declan. Hi!" Her eyes widen with surprise and excitement and I want to throw up. She completely forgets about me, bumping me out of the way as she steps closer to Declan.

Rolling my eyes, I turn and head toward the bar. The two of them can have each other. Drowning my emotions in a drink seems like the better option right now anyways. I order three shots, two whiskey sours, and a beer for Roger.

I wait as the bartender prepares my order, turning to see Jillian still chatting it up with Declan. Just watching her as she practically fawns over Declan makes me want to claw her eyes out. I watch as her hand runs down his arm, and I want to rip it from her body.

God, him being back in town makes me fucking violent.

"Might wanna fix your face." Nicole steps in front of me, blocking my view of the two of them. I didn't even know she'd walked in, I'd been so fixated on him I wasn't paying attention to anything else. "You're not hiding your feelings well."

I turn back to the bar just as the bartender sets the shots down, grabbing one of them, I toss it back and grunt as the liquid burns on the way down.

Fucking *bitch*.

Not my best friend, but Jillian. Granted, Nicole's a bitch too for making me do this shit tonight.

Jillian wanted Declan in high school, and clearly that hasn't changed based on the way she's attempting to climb him right now.

Okay, that's a little far stretched, but I'm sure she sounds like a fucking purring cat waiting to be mated with.

Shaking my head, I grab another shot and down it, not giving a damn about who's watching. When I sit it back down, I look at Nicole whose eyes are wide, bouncing from me to the glass.

Shit.

"Can I get two more of those?" I bite at my bottom lip.

How in the hell does he get under my skin like this? Enough to make me throw back two shots and order another round since I'm drinking the ones I ordered for my friends. Glancing over my shoulder, I'm met with his blue eyes, swimming with an emotion that I can't quite place.

It's almost pity, but something more.

"Here you go." The bartender places our drinks on a tray to make it easier for me to carry.

I purposely avoid looking in Declan's direction but can feel his eyes on me as I cross the gym to the table Roger is sitting at. Nicole sits beside her husband, while I take the open seat next to her.

"At least we can legally drink at these events now." Nicole raises her shot glass, Roger and I do the same. We used to sneak alcohol into the school dances, and no one ever noticed. Then we'd leave and go walk around the park at night, watching the moon above us as we laughed with each other.

I miss those days. More than I'd like to admit.

"Those were the days." I tip my glass back, coughing slightly at the taste and burn. "How did no one notice what we were doing?"

"Hell if I know. I wouldn't trust a teenager at all after all the shit we did in school." She laughs.

All I can think about is Lane and Lucy at school dances in the future and I cringe at the thought. Lane is going to wreak havoc on this school, Kyle wasn't a walk in the park and his son is the mini version of him. And Lucy? Well, the jury is still out on her. She's sweet like her momma, but she has that wild streak to her like her daddy.

The seat next to me screeches against the gym floor as it's pulled back, turning my attention to the person next to me. I groan in frustration when I see Declan taking a seat. He smiles, sitting his beer on the table and leaning back in his chair. My eyes dart to the name plate that I hadn't noticed sitting next to me.

That bitch, Jillian. She planned this shit perfectly to try to ruin my night.

"It's just like old times."

I bristle at his choice of words, fighting the heartache that hits me in the chest hard. Nicole notices and reaches under the table, squeezing my knee in support.

I ignore him, choosing to focus on what the hell I've done wrong throughout my life to deserve this type of karma.

And by karma, I mean having Jillian Baker in charge of the damn seating arrangement.

17

DECLAN

AFTER PRYING Jillian off of me, I head toward the bar for a beer. Everytime I see Lou and the way that fucking dress clings to her body, I find myself needing something to take the damn edge off. When I walked in and saw her, my mouth watered at the sight. She looks beautiful, and that alone makes the ache in my chest grow. It never went away, always there reminding me of what a fuck up I am and everything I threw away.

I grab the beer placed on the bar and take a long pull, letting it fight away the pain I'm experiencing. My eyes move around the room, seeking her out. They always go to her, *always*.

I find her, almost instantly, sitting next to Nicole and her husband. Her head tips back slightly in laughter. She's so goddamn beautiful and doesn't even know it.

I walk in her direction when it's announced to find our seats. Groaning in frustration at the timing, I start looking around for my designated seat, greeting a few people I went to school with in the process. Finally, I find my name, and it just so happens to be right next to Lou's.

I'm coming for you, baby.

I grab the chair next to hers, pulling it back slowly as it grates against the gym floor beneath my feet. Nicole's eyes shift to mine in surprise, but she doesn't say anything. Roger tilts his head in greeting but focuses on his beer. Three empty shot glasses sit on the table next to some type of table decoration with balloons attached to the top.

Her head turns in my direction, ready to greet whoever is sitting next to her, a large smile on her face that fades as soon as she sees it's me. I wish I could say that didn't hurt, but it sure as fuck does.

I'm guessing she didn't read the name plates when she sat down. I don't know who placed the two of us next to each other, but I'm sure thankful right now that they did.

"It's just like old times." I grin, taking another drink of my beer.

Her attention turns back to Nicole, ignoring what I've said completely. Jillian takes the stage, standing in the center and looks over in my direction. Her wink is seen by everyone in the room and it makes me want to gag. She's always been interested, she never hid it, and it used to drive Lou up the wall. I'm guessing it still does based on the way Lou side-eye's me with a snarl on her lips.

Jillian's voice echoes throughout the gym. She talks about high school, and how things have changed. She can't believe how quickly time has passed, and that's one thing I agree with her on.

"It's been wonderful mingling with everyone so far," she says. "Seeing how successful *some* have been in their lives."

Her eyes cut over to Lou, and I fight back the urge to say something to defend Lou.

Lou doesn't show that it bothers her, but I know it does. Jillian was always able to get under her skin, but Lou always wore a strong face and tried to never let it bother her.

Until Jillian kept trying to bum a ride home with me, then Lou snapped. It was the best fucking thing, and she looked sexy as hell telling Jillian to stay the fuck away from her man in the student parking lot.

"We've compiled a video from our high school years, but first, let's toast to our bright, *successful* futures." She lifts her drink of whatever wine she's sipping on into the air. Lou lifts her whiskey sour, taking a small drink while I do the same with my beer, then everyone takes a quick drink. I chuckle at the fact that Lou takes a large drink, and then one more sip before she sits it on the table.

The lights are turned low, the only thing lit up in the room now is the large projector shining against the wall behind where Jillian was just standing. Everyone turns their seats so they can get a better view. Our class song begins, and I can't say the emotions don't hit me. It starts with a few shots of our freshman year.

I was a scrawny mother fucker back then. I laugh at one of the shots of me in agriculture class, holding a plant up as the picture was taken. Lou looks away when she sees me, and I immediately hate that I still cause her so much pain.

Leaning toward her, my shoulder brushes against hers and it burns through my blazer like a branding iron. That's what she is after all, branded into me. A thought, a memory, a feeling that I can't erase.

"You look beautiful tonight," I whisper, and watch as chill bumps break out over her arm. I smile, wider than I have in a long fucking time knowing that I still have this type of affect on her. "I didn't get a chance to tell you earlier."

Her head tilts in my direction, but she doesn't respond. Instead, she turns her attention back to the screen where a picture of her and Nicole flash across the screen in their cheerleading uniforms. I smile to myself, remembering just how much I loved that skirt on her.

"So," I say, pulling her attention back to me. "Where's Tim?" Her head jerks in my direction, brows pinched together before she recovers and smooths out her features.

"He's working, couldn't make it." She shrugs. She says it so quickly, I know it's a fucking lie.

"How long have y'all been together?" I'm curious, even though I don't think the two of them are together. I know my girl couldn't let go of that grudge so easily. Especially not to the point of dating him. Then I remind myself that I don't know this Lou at all. The girl from high school still may be in there, but this one is new.

My voice blares through the speaker, pulling my attention from Lou to the screen. My time capsule video is playing. I forgot all about recording these, it was right before my dad passed away and I thought my future was fucking golden. I had the girl, and that's all I cared about.

"Where do you see yourself in ten years?" Jillian asks.

"Honestly?" I laugh, running a hand over my face to hide my smile. "I'll be married to Lou Tucker, except she won't be Tucker anymore." I shake my head, my smile growing. "She'll be Mrs. Declan Sanchez then.

We'll have two kids, a boy and a girl. They'll be perfect, just like her."

"That's sweet, but like where do you see yourself? Like you, not Lou."

"That's all I see." I look at the camera. "All I see in my future is Lou."

The camera cuts off, rolling to another person's film. We all sit in silence, watching each video and remembering how easily things change. I remember how I felt when filming that, how that was the only thing on my mind.

Just Lou.

Not my dad. Not my career choices. Hell, college didn't even fucking matter.

Just her.

Lou's video starts playing. Her long blonde hair was pulled into a low ponytail that day, just the way I liked it. And still do.

"Where do you see yourself in ten years?" Jillian asks. "Standard question." Her tone is different than she used in my video but Lou doesn't let it bother her.

"In ten years, I'll be a nurse working for the local hospital. I want to help people, and I think it's the perfect option for me. Plus, it'll be a good job for when Declan and I get married. We'll have a family by then, I hope." She laughs. "It'll be perfect."

Her words hit me in the chest so hard, I have to lean back and rub at the spot. I wanted that too, baby. *More than you know.*

"Yeah, sounds exciting." Jillian pushes past her lips.

The screen cuts off again, rolling to another student. Without thinking, I reach out and touch the back of her arm, trying to express what I'm feeling in that touch. She sucks in a deep breath and jumps to her feet, running out of the room.

Nicole glances from me to her retreating form, then back to me with a look that could set me on fire. She slowly stands, sitting her glass on the table and follows after Lou.

Fuck. I stand, and follow after them both.

18

LOU

As soon as the cool air fills my lungs, I feel like I can breathe again.

The video was too much, hearing his words nearly gutted me, but hearing mine and what I wanted for myself was something entirely different.

I thought I could do this tonight, that coming here would bring me some type of closure from that part of my life, but all it's done is pour salt into an ever growing wound. I've never felt pain like this before, not even when he left me.

This is a type of pain that I wouldn't even wish on Jillian, and I can't stand that bitch at all. This pain is the type that consumes you, and him being here only adds to it.

I hate it. And I hate him for making me feel it.

I focus on my breathing, trying to fight back the tears because the last thing I need is for Jillian to come out here and see me falling apart. That's one thing I won't give that bitch, is the satisfaction of watching me break.

The door behind me swings open as Nicole steps into the night air beside me. Her face is full of concern as she looks me over to make sure I'm okay.

"Hi." she says, stepping closer to me. "You okay?"

"No," I laugh, even though none of this is funny. "Not even a little."

"Oh, Lou." She wraps her arm around me. "Do you want to leave?"

"No." *Yes.* That's what I really want to say, but my pride won't allow me to walk away and give in to Jillian. "I'll be okay, I just need to catch my breath. That was... a lot."

"Yeah, I had forgotten all about those time capsules. If it makes you feel any better, I was talking about that guy I was talking to from Sun Crest." We both laugh. "That was awkward while I was sitting with my husband."

"I bet." She makes me laugh again, and the mood lightens a little.

Until Declan steps through the door, his eyes lasering in on mine. His lips are pursed as he steps closer to me, searching my face for any emotion that I may give him.

And no matter how much I fight it, a tear falls anyways.

Declan steps closer, not caring that Nicole has an arm around my shoulder. His thumb rises, wiping away the lone tear while looking into my eyes with an emotion I've never experienced from him.

"I'm going to, um, go check on Roger. Are you okay?"

I nod, but don't look at her, I can't. The man in front of me has captivated my attention. There's one thing I need to know, and I wait until she walks inside before asking the question.

"Why?" It's a simple word, one that I've been waiting to say for years but never thought I'd get the chance to ask.

His shoulders fall, and he cuts the moment we just had and takes a step away from me. I already miss his closeness, and that scares the shit out of me.

I stare at him as he runs a hand through his hair, as he turns away and stops next to the brick beside the door. His arm reaches above him, resting against the brick while his other shoves into his pocket.

"I just need to know why," I beg.

"I–" He pauses, clearing his throat.

I can't see his face, but I can tell he's struggling to get the words out. I take a step closer to him, my shoe brushing across the pavement causes him to look over his shoulder.

"After my dad died, I felt like I needed to join to feel closer to him." He's still not looking at me, but I remain silent letting him get out what he's trying to say. "I never wanted to hurt you, Lou." He turns, facing me. I'm not sure why, but I believe those words when they fall from his lips. His eyes are pleading for me to understand. "That was the last thing I wanted to do, but I couldn't put you in the situation that I've watched my mom live my entire life. Every time my dad left, I saw it rip her apart with fear, and I refused to let you live that life. It was stupid, and a mistake, but I couldn't let you live that life."

His words sink in, bringing up an emotion that is no longer hatred for the man standing in front of me, but something entirely different. "Why didn't you just tell me that?"

"How could I? You wouldn't have understood, at least not from my standpoint on it all. You would have told me that you'd be able to handle it." His eyes study mine. He's right, I would have told him anything to keep him from leaving me then. "But I couldn't do that to you. I couldn't leave knowing that you were here falling apart every single day that I wasn't with you."

But that's what happened. I fell apart more with each passing moment he was gone.

"That was my choice to make though, Declan. I've spent the last fifteen years thinking I did something to make you not love me anymore, that it was my fault and I somehow drove you away." I choke on my words, my emotions coming out in full force.

"No, baby." He steps closer to me, grabbing my face in his hands as he pulls me against his body. "It was never you, this was all me. You did nothing wrong, you were fucking perfect, Lou. You still are."

I look into his eyes, listening to his words and letting them wrap around me to heal a part of me that only he can heal.

"I loved you so much then that I had to let you go, I couldn't take you down with me and that's where I was heading. *Down,*" he stresses. "I lost myself, and I didn't want you to see any of that happen," he whispers.

Loved.

That's the only word I heard. He loved me, past tense, which means he doesn't love me now.

"Stop it."

I jerk my eyes back to his.

"Stop focusing on that word."

How does he know that's what I was doing?

"I still love you, Lou. I haven't dated anyone since you, because no one fucking compared. My feelings for you never changed, not once. I still have our pictures in my wallet." He releases me, reaching into his back pocket and pulls out his wallet. The same one he had when we were teenagers, except now the leather is worn around the edges and not the same golden brown it once was.

He flips it open and there's our prom picture, the one from the night he told me he was going to marry me.

"I–" I pause, trying to find my words. "I don't know what to say."

"You don't have to say anything, baby. Just know that I'm sorry." He puts his wallet away, looking into my eyes once he's finished. My tears have slowed, but he still wipes the wetness from under my eyes and I can't help but lean into his touch. "I'm so sorry, baby."

Without thinking, I wrap my arms around his waist and he engulfs me with his, providing that same sense of safety I felt all those years ago every time he held me.

I don't know how long we stay like this, but I don't want to let the moment go. I can't. I've waited years for this closure, but I still don't feel like I'm whole again.

A noise from inside pulls me from my thoughts, the music playing is some that I recognize from our high school dances. I laugh, and he drops his arms from around me.

"You want to leave? I can drop you off at home," he offers.

God, do I want to... I really fucking do, but I can't.

"No." I straighten my dress and wipe under my eyes, praying I don't look like a disaster after my cry fest. "I refuse to let Jillian see me leave like this."

He chuckles, the sound going straight to my vagina. "No, we can't." He smiles, offering his arm to me.

I hesitate, but take it, feeling like I can finally under-stand why he did what he did. Even though I don't agree with his decision, or how he did everything... at least I know why.

19

DECLAN

WALKING with her on my arm brings me all the memories of our past. A past filled with memories both happy and painful that I never thought we'd overcome, but yet, here she is, holding on to me as every eye in the gym turns in our direction.

This is how it was always supposed to be. The two of us, together and smiling.

Jillian is dancing with a few people at the center of the gym floor, she halts as soon as she realizes something has caught everyone's attention. It doesn't take long for her smile to fade when she sees the two of us together. I'm enjoying this more than anyone knows right now, and I know Lou is too.

The song switches, and as soon as it does I recognize it. The tempo is the perfect mix between fast and slow before the words beat from the speakers.

Chasing Cars by Snow Patrol.

I used to dance with Lou to this every time it came on. It didn't matter if we were on a gravel road in the middle of nowhere, I'd stop the truck, crank the volume up as high as I could and leave the doors open before pulling her in front of my truck and wrapping her in my arms.

"Wanna dance?" I ask, spinning so I'm in front of her.

She looks up at me, tears filling her eyes again and I fight back the urge to kiss her, because, God, do I want to right now. I don't know where her head is with everything I've told her a few minutes ago.

Knowing her, she'd probably knock the shit out of me.

Everyone is still staring when she looks away from me, and it's then that I see how nervous she is. It's been fifteen years since we've done anything like this, and now every eye in the room is focused on the two of us and what this means.

I don't even know what *this* means, but I do know one thing.

I want her, and I want to work on whatever is left between us. If that's something she chooses to do. The last thing I expected when I came home was for the two of us to rekindle any old flame we had. My therapist had one goal in mind, and that was to get my head straight. That required me getting things off my chest to Lou about why I left.

I've done that now, but I'm not done with her. *I could never be done with her.*

Leaning forward until my lips are hovering just above her ear, I whisper, "It's just the two of us, no one else, baby."

She's silent for a second before the slight tilt of her head gives me the okay I've been waiting on. I lead her to the dance floor, spinning her to face me when we reach the center and pull her into my arms. I hold her close, like I've dreamed of doing all this time. Her ear is pressed against my chest, and I know that even with the bass blaring the way it is right now, she can still hear and feel my heart pounding in my chest.

Nicole and her husband watch from our table, their eyes never leaving us. I can see Nicole biting her bottom lip, nervous due to the two of us together like this. I'm sure she's wondering the same thing we are, *what are we doing?*

I hold Lou against my body, basking in the feeling of how her body molds perfectly against mine. Her head stays in its place against my chest while my hands are linked behind her. I'm trying to figure out what's going through that gorgeous head of hers, but I can't.

Once the song ends, she pulls away from me but doesn't release me. I look down at her, trying to gauge what she wants to do next, but her words surprise me.

"I'm ready to go now." She smiles.

I lead her toward the table where Nicole and Roger are sitting. Nicole eyes me cautiously, just like a best friend should. I know she's worried about this, and I don't fucking blame her. But I'm glad that Lou has had her over the years, they've always had a friendship that was unlike anything I've ever seen before.

"Hey," Lou shouts over the deafening music. "We're going to head out."

"Okay, let's go," Nicole says, standing and grabbing her husband's hand.

I suck in a breath as my nerves rise, I hadn't thought of the fact that she wouldn't actually be leaving with me, she did come with them after all, or that's what I gathered.

"No." She shakes her head and holds a hand up to halt her friends. "I'm going with Declan." Her eyes slide to mine and I can't help but smile down at her. "You stay, enjoy the rest of your night," Lou tells her.

I relax, biting back the smile that starts to form.

"You sure?" Nicole looks from Lou to me.

"Positive." Lou glances over her shoulder, winking at me before continuing. "We talked, it's okay. I'll call you tomorrow." She lets go of my hand and hugs her best friend before kissing Roger on the cheek. "Have fun."

When she turns to face me, I catch the glare from Nicole's eyes before she narrows them in a look that very easily conveys that she'll chop my balls off if I hurt her. I nod in response, message received.

Loud and fucking clear.

All eyes watch us once again as we head for the exit, I don't stop, not telling anyone goodbye and when Jillian attempts to stop me, I brush her off like she doesn't matter.

Because she doesn't, the only one that ever has is under my arm.

But Lou stops, ducking under my arm and causing me to brake to figure out what the fuck is going on. She's standing right in front of Jillian, her eyes flashing with that same fire I used to see years ago.

"I hope you have a goodnight, Jillian." She smiles, looking back at me. "Declan and I will."

With that, she turns, nearly slapping Jillian in the face with her hair. I smirk, feeling damn good about the way this night is going to end, and praying that she's not just going to ask me to drive her home. Although, the way the night has gone is far better than I imagined it to be so far.

"Where too?" I ask, opening my truck door for her.

"My brother's bar?"

I start to object, to tell her that I don't think it's a good idea that we go there.

"He's not working tonight, he's home."

"Alright." I smile, ushering her in but only shutting the door once she's buckled, a habit that clearly hasn't been broken with her.

Neither one of us speak on the way to the bar, but she does hold my hand on the drive so that's a good sign right? Plus, she hasn't said she wants to go home yet.

Once we walk in, she waves at the bartender working and he nods before she leads me to a table near the back. She sits, crossing her legs once she's situated while I hang my blazer over the back of my chair before taking my own seat.

Two beers are placed in front of us, and the guy bends to place a kiss on her cheek. My jaw ticks, the jealousy coming on strong because I don't know this son of a bitch, but Lou doesn't seem to react to it and I don't really have a leg to stand on here, I don't have the right to be jealous.

"So, when did your brother open this place?" I take a drink of my beer, looking around the bar.

"A few years ago, he's done really well with it." She smiles, proud of her brother's accomplishments as she looks around the bar.

"It's nice." I nod, watching as she tilts the bottle to her lips. I stare as she swallows, finding it hard to pull my attention to anything else right now. "So, he's married now?"

"He is. Tessa." She digs in her purse thingy that she brought, I don't know what you call it. It doesn't have straps, and it buttons in the front. Her phone materializes and she flicks through something before turning it so I can see. "These are his kids, they're twins. Tessa's in the back."

"Beautiful family." I look at the little girl, she reminds me of Lou in some ways, but that little boy is the spitting image of his father.

"I love being an aunt." She gushes, looking down at the picture.

I smile at her, but that same sense of hurt hits me again. I should be their uncle, that's how it was always going to go. They should be calling me Uncle Declan, and having sleepovers with our own kids.

"So, you bought the clinic?" Her eyes widen slightly. "Aunt B. told me about it." I take a drink of my beer. "Proud of you."

"Thanks." She turns her head to look out at the dance floor. "I love what I do."

All I can do is smile at her. I'm so proud of her, she went above and beyond with her dreams.

After a few drinks, we hit the dance floor and both of us are feeling the buzz from the alcohol and decide it's time we head out.

"How far away are you?" I ask once we step outside, the cool air causing chill bumps on her skin. I wrap my blazer in my hand around her shoulders and watch as she slowly stops shaking.

"Just a few blocks, we could probably walk if you wanted." She bites her bottom lip. Is that an invitation?

I look down at her feet, staring at the heels she's wearing. "Are you good at walking in those while intoxicated?"

"I'll take them off." She bends, releasing the straps and sliding her feet out.

The ground has to be cold underneath her bare feet,

and when her foot hits the concrete, the hiss I hear tells me what I need to know. Stepping forward, I bend, grabbing behind her back and knees and lift her against my chest, making sure that no one that passes us will get a view of what's under this dress.

"I can walk."

"I know you can." I smirk down at her, and wait for her to point me in the direction we need to go. "But I like you here."

She smiles up at me before pointing in the direction of her house, I head that way, holding her tightly against me. It's not lost on me that I may be heading back this direction in a few minutes, but for now I'm enjoying having her this close to me.

"You always were such a gentleman," she whispers, wrapping her arms around my neck and getting comfortable in my arms.

"Only with you." I look down and kiss the tip of her nose. I don't know why I do it, but I do. She doesn't act like it bothers her, so I relax slightly and listen to her talk.

"That's a lie, you were always a gentleman." She lays her head against my chest and continues to point me in the direction of her house.

When we reach her driveway, she assures me she can walk so I stop in front of her garage door and set her down. She flips the exterior controller open and taps on a few buttons before it opens. I remain standing where I am, not wanting her to think I'm pressuring her into inviting me in but sure as fuck hoping she does.

Her eyes meet mine, and they tell me enough to know that I should follow her.

20

DECLAN

I'M TRYING SO HARD NOT ACT like a fucking teenage boy with the excitement of going to a girls house. But that's exactly what I am... fucking giddy.

Stepping toward her, she giggles but turns and heads for the entrance to her house. She pushes the door open, and I want to say something about it being unlocked but don't get the chance because I'm pushed against the wall as soon as the door shuts.

Her fingers move through my hair, pulling and tugging as her lips press against mine. My hands move to her ass as I lift her in my arms and spin us both so that she's the one against the wall now. She starts working her pussy up and down against the length of my hardened cock.

My fingers curl underneath the fabric of her black dress, digging into her flesh when she rocks against me.

"Fuck," I breathe.

She releases me, dropping her legs to the ground. I'm nervous for a few short moments until I realize she's unzipping the side of her dress. She pulls her arms free and lets the fabric fall from her hips, leaving her in nothing but a black lace bra and a matching thong.

Fuck me.

Her body's changed, but in a good fucking way. She has curves that beg me to reach out and follow with my hands, and honestly I prefer this version of her.

Her toned legs step out of the fabric pooled at her feet. I drink her in, letting my eyes roam over every inch of her bare skin. I'm about to ask where the bedroom is when she jumps at me, kissing me like we may never get this chance again. Like she's been waiting years for this moment, and I know I fucking have.

I lift her again, her ankles lock around my waist with her sex rubbing against the bulge in my pants that shows her exactly how much I want her. My grip tightens on her ass, so hard that I almost think I'm hurting her until she moans into my mouth. The way she pulls my hair makes me think she's enjoying every bit of what she's getting right now.

"Are you sure about this?" I pant, pulling back slightly so I can look in her eyes. I need to hear her say it, to hear her give the okay that this is what she wants to happen between us right now.

She nods. "God, yes."

I grin, bringing my lips down to hers once more. "Where's the bedroom?"

She points toward a hallway, and I follow her directions until I come to the master bedroom and push the door open. Her place is nice, at least from what I've seen of it so far. I know I walked through the main living area, but my focus is on the beautiful woman in my arms, driving me fucking crazy with the way she's rubbing against me with each step I take.

I step inside, not stopping until my knees hit the edge of her bed. I slowly lay her against the comforter, going up on my arms, moving my lower body so I can get a look at her. Her eyes flash before her red nails skate down her abdomen toward her panties. When her thumbs hook in either side and slowly start to slide them off, I have to bite my bottom lip for restraint.

I'm seconds away from fucking drooling over this girl, and she isn't even completely bare to me yet.

"Do you have a condom?" she asks, pulling her panties free from her legs.

"Fuck," I growl. "I wasn't expecting this..."

"It's okay, I'm on the pill," she says, tossing her panties to the side. "Are you clean?"

I freeze.

I've never done this, been inside of anyone without one. I've never wanted to before, but right now, it's all I fucking want to do.

"Passed a physical not even three weeks ago. It's been a while since I've been with anyone."

She grins, but I can see the wheels turning at the idea of me being with anyone else swirling in her mind. I've been with others, but only as an itch to scratch. They never meant anything to me, it was always Lou I pictured. I have to fight the anger bubbling inside of me at the thought of her and her fucking ex that my mom was talking about.

"What about Tim?" I ask, grinning as his name slips from my lips. Knowing the entire thing has been a ruse.

"Oh, shut up." She swats my arm. "You know we aren't

together." She rolls her eyes, spreading her legs further apart, giving me the perfect view of her pink pussy. "Now fuck me."

You don't have to tell me twice, baby. I've been fucking waiting years for this moment.

My hands move to my belt, undoing it before popping the button of my slacks. She leans up on her elbows, sliding the straps of her bra down her arms before reaching behind her and unhooking the clasp. I grin, watching her movement as I push my slacks and underwear past my hips.

My cock bursts free, slapping against her pussy and causing us both to groan at the feeling.

"Christ," she breathes, letting her hand wrap around my length. "I forgot how big you are."

I bend, pressing a kiss to her lips before pulling away and stepping out of my pants and underwear. Reaching forward, I hook my hands around her hips and bring her pussy to my lips. Her surprised gasp causes me to smile before my tongue slowly glides through her lips.

I groan at the taste of her. Fuck, have I missed this taste. I start to lap at her entrance, swallowing her juices as my nose presses against her clit. Her hands are securely latched onto my hair, using it to guide my tongue further into her.

Just when she starts to moan, I pull away, breaking all contact. The look on her face makes me chuckle before I start to crawl back over her. She bites her bottom lip, slowly pulling her body up the mattress until she's resting against the comfort of her pillows.

I shuffle forward on my knees until my cock slides across her sex. She thinks I'm going to sink in like this, but she's wrong.

She's forgetting that I have every single pleasurable touch her body enjoys memorized. And I've thought about her sweet moans every fucking day since I walked away from her.

I grab her ankles, flipping her so that she's on her stomach before reaching under her and bringing her ass to the air. My hand fists her hair, pulling it slightly like I know she likes and when the sound of bliss slips from her lips, my dick pulses with need.

"Please, baby," she begs, wiggling her ass at me.

I move forward, the head of my dick finding her entrance and slide all the way in. The feeling is so intense that I could come right now.

She's so fucking tight, that I have to stop myself, unable to move the sensation so strong. Her pussy swallows my dick, sucking it all the way in to the hilt. She presses her ass back against me, urging me to move. Her pussy is unlike anything I've ever experienced, and I don't intend to let it go again.

I plan to tell her that as soon as I'm done showing her.

Pumping my hips, her pussy squeezes my cock so tight that I swear I see stars. "You feel fucking amazing."

She laughs, causing her core to contract and her pussy to clamp down so tight that I have to suck in a breath. I won't last five minutes like this, what the fuck was I thinking. I knew this was my weakness when I flipped her over, it always has been. It's the curve of her back and the way her ass presses against me while I pump inside of he that drives me fucking mad.

I pull out, resting on my ankles as she groans in frustration. I've cut her off from pleasure twice now, and if I know my girl, she's getting really pissed off about it right now.

"Declan, so help me God."

I laugh at her words, watching as she rolls to her back. I lean over her, looking into her eyes before slowly sliding in this time. I watch as her face changes with each inch I give her until I'm in all the way.

Her pussy's slicker than before, and I don't know how that's even possible. I move against her again, not breaking eye contact as I do. The urge to watch as she falls apart under me is strong.

Whatever's passing between us right now is felt by both of us. A tear starts to form in the corner of her eye, I lean down pressing my lips to hers again and rock my hips harder against her until she convulses. Her pleasured screams send me over the edge, ripping through me unlike anything I've felt before.

My arms give out, but I somehow manage to catch myself before crashing against her body and move off to the side as my dick slips free.

"How do you do that?" she asks, breathlessly.

"Do what?"

"Make it feel better each time."

I snort. "Same goes for you, baby."

She laughs and turns to her side so that she's facing me. I do the same, draping an arm over her waist. We stare at each other for a long moment before she shifts so her body is against mine and rests her head against my chest. I pull the comforter from beneath us, trying not to mess up our position and pull it over our naked bodies.

I've wanted this moment for so long, I missed it. The feel of her body against mine as we lay together. Granted, most of the time our bodies were like this in high school, in the back of my truck, but I missed it.

The pounding of my heart against her cheek is soothing as I run my other hand through her curled hair. I press my lips against her head, she leans her head back until she can see my eyes.

I look down at her, studying her eyes. "Will you stay tonight?"

"I don't ever want to let you go again, Lou."

A small smile spreads across her lips before she settles back in against me.

I don't ever want to be without her again.

21

LOU

My eyes flutter open, the morning light sneaking in from the curtains that aren't fully pulled shut. I'm cold as I roll to my back, feeling the comforter slide across my bare skin.

My mind flashes to what we did last night, when I look to his side of the bed, it's empty. The pillow is turned slightly and a note is sitting on top of it with his handwriting on the front.

My stomach sinks. Did he leave? What did I do wrong? I thought he was into what happened between us last night.

Sitting up, I pull the covers over my chest and grab the piece of paper to read. Taking a slow deep breath, I blow it out before unfolding it and reading what he's written.

Baby,

Sorry I had to leave, have a few things to take care of this morning and didn't want to wake you. You were so beautiful.

I meant what I said last night, I don't ever want to lose you again.

Text me when you wake up.
Dec

I smile as I read his words, feeling relieved that he didn't leave, not in the way I had thought he did. But, I'm hoping and praying that what he's saying is true. That he doesn't want to lose me again, but there's still that voice in the back of my head reminding me of what happened the last time I gave myself to him.

Looking at the number he's left at the bottom of the note, I type it into my phone. I'm about to send a quick message letting him know that I'm up when I hear a knock on my door. Standing, I grab a shirt from the closet and a pair of gym shorts before heading to answer it.

Just as I'm coming out of my room, my front door opens and I freeze in fear. Nicole comes into view and I swear, I want to beat the hell out of her. But then I remember, I'd have to beat the hell out of myself for giving her a key.

"Holy shit." I slap my hand to my chest, trying to slow my rapid breaths. "Remind me to take that fucking key from you."

She jumps. She fucking jumps like I'm just the one that scared the shit out of her.

"Sorry." She relaxes. "I wasn't sure if you were up or not..." She looks over my shoulder into the bedroom. "Or alone for that matter."

"So, what? You were going to waltz in there and catch a show?" I laugh.

"God, I wish. Roger and I fell asleep as soon as we got home. We were so tired and rarely get nights out without coming home to the kids."

She's right, they hardly ever do anything date night

wise. I offer to watch her kids often, but she declines because she feels guilty.

She turns toward my kitchen and that's when I see the bags in her hands, the local bakery logo stamped on the front.

"*Oh*," I groan, mouth already watering at what could be in the bag. "Please tell me there's a cinnamon roll in there," I beg.

"What kind of friend do you think I am?" She tosses a bag in my direction. "There's two." She winks before sitting the drink carrier on the island. "Plus your favorite coffee."

"You're an angel," I tell her, taking the cup and smelling the aroma that only coffee offers.

"And you're a little vixen. Tell me what happened last night."

I blush, my mind jumping to what happened between Declan and I last night.

"I knew it," she says, pointing at me. "I fucking knew it. You fucked him didn't you?"

"I–"

"You don't have to say anything, hoe." She giggles. "It's written all over your face... and hair, based on the tangles you're sporting this morning."

I pat at my head, watching as her smile grows wider.

"Give me all the details." She grabs my arm and pulls me forward, shoving my chair out so I can sit.

I take another drink, needing the caffeine before I start.

"When we left last night, we decided to head to the bar."

Her eyes widen.

"Kyle wasn't working last night," I hurry to explain.

There is no way in hell I would have gone there if he had been on shift. That would have ruined the night before it even got started. And after everything that happened during the reunion, I needed more time with him. I can't explain it, I just needed to be close to him.

I sure as hell didn't expect the night to turn out the way it did, but I'm not complaining now.

"Oh, whew. That would have been a disaster."

"I know, which is why I made sure to check that Kyle was off work."

She waves her hand between us, urging me to continue with the story. "Okay. Go on."

"Anyways, we just drank and danced. By the time we decided to leave, both of us were too buzzed to drive so we walked back to my place." I smirk, thinking of the walk home. "Well," I tilt my head, "he walked, while carrying me. My heels were killing me and the ground was cold."

"Oh, gosh." She leans forward, resting her elbow on her knee and propping her chin up on her fist. "I forgot how sweet he can be." Her words make me smile.

"Then we came back here, and..." I bite my bottom lip, feeling my face flush.

"Oh my gosh, look at you. I haven't seen you like this in a long time, babe." She reaches over, touching my arm before giving a gentle squeeze. "What did he say when I went back inside last night?"

"He basically told me that he joined because he felt it was a way to be closer to his dad." Saying that breaks my heart, that he felt he had to join to be closer to his dad. I didn't know what he was going through back then, I still don't honestly. I've never lost anyone like that, but it breaks my heart for him all over again. "And that he broke up with me because he didn't want to think about me going through the same thing his mom went through every time his dad was deployed," I explain.

"Ugh, why does this man make it so hard to hate him?" She rolls her eyes, taking a drink of her own coffee.

"I wish I knew." Because after everything last night, while I don't agree with his decisions of the past, I forgive him. I'm still leery of him, because that heartache isn't something I ever want to experience again, but I forgive him.

"Did you see Jillian's face when you told her to enjoy her night and mentioned that the two of you would?"

I shake my head, I didn't bother waiting around to see her reaction, but I hope it was a good one.

"Oh, my God. It was the best. I bet her jaw drug across the ground for a solid thirty minutes after that."

"Good, serves her fucking right." I tear into my cinnamon roll, not caring if the frosting smears across my face. I'm not impressing anyone right now.

"So what does this mean for the two of you?" she asks, taking a bite of her bagel.

"I honestly don't know, we didn't talk about any of that. He was gone when I woke up but left a note saying that he didn't want to lose me again."

Nicole swoons in front of me. "Ugh, I hate to love him."

We both laugh. She stays for another hour before needing to get home for her kids. I have some charts to work on that I didn't get to last week, so I spend the rest of my day getting caught up for the work week.

———

Walking into work the next day, I feel lighter. Which sounds ridiculous but I don't know how else to describe it. It's like a weight has been lifted from my shoulders, one that I've carried for years. My smile's a little brighter, and I've caught myself smiling several times for no reason other than thinking about my night with Declan.

We talked before I went to bed last night, he offered to come by but I was so deep in charting from being off work Friday and not getting anything done that I needed to and I didn't want to ruin the vibe I had... and that's exactly what would have happened if he'd come over. We'd have gotten distracted by each other and ended up right back in bed.

"You have a new patient first thing this morning, but then you only have a few more. Pretty easy day, I'm still trying to get a few from last week rescheduled, so it may fill up," Talia tells me as I walk past her desk.

"Thanks, girl." I smile as she answers the ringing phone.

I hurry to my office, depositing my bag and grabbing my white coat before heading to the new patient's exam room. My phone buzzes, halting my steps. I walk back around my desk and hit the speaker button.

"Hey, Lou. I have Autumn Baker on the line. I was hoping I'd catch you before you walked into your first appointment. I had tried to call Autumn a few days ago to check in with her but didn't get through.

"Put her through." I smile and pull my chair away from my desk to sit.

When the phone rings, I pick it up and hold it against

my ear. "Autumn." I grin through the phone. "How are you feeling?"

"I'm good." She pauses and I hear a soft cry, bringing another smile to my lips. "We're good." She laughs.

We talk a little longer about how the baby is doing and how she has been feeling. She's nearly two and a half weeks postpartum, but sounds good. Before I transfer her back to the front so Talia can schedule her six week postpartum appointment, I make her promise to call if there are any changes.

Feeling better about my day, I grab one of the iPads and start reviewing her chart as I get closer to the room.

Knocking before pushing the door open, I smile when I step inside and see a young couple holding hands. "Goodmorning, I'm Dr. Tucker." I approach them both, shaking their hands. They greet me, introducing themselves. "Is this your first pregnancy?" I ask.

"Yes, ma'am," the woman says, looking over at her partner with a big smile.

"Alright, let's cover some of the basics." I go over everything they should expect from their visits and provide them with health information, including what medications she is able to take right now and what she should steer clear of.

Once we're finished, she heads off to the lab to have her blood drawn while I head back to the nurses' station. A few of the nurses are busy but one approaches, handing me an iPad with labs pulled up.

"Here's the lab results from the Wheatley family." Her tone of voice worrying me.

"Damn," I whisper, scrolling through the file. "She's having a miscarriage."

The nurse nods. "Yes."

"Can you call them? Schedule an appointment for today."

She nods, taking the tablet back.

This is the part of my job that I absolutely hate the most. Having to tell someone they're losing their baby.

I grip the edge of the counter, squeezing my eyes shut tightly while I fight away the emotions that are overpowering me right now. It never gets easier, ever. Someone standing at the front desk catches my attention, and when I narrow my eyes to get a clear view of who it is, I roll my eyes before pushing away from the nurses' station and walking in that direction.

"What are you doing here?" I ask Peter.

He turns when he hears my voice and shoves his hands in his pocket.

"I just wanted to talk, do you have a minute?"

Glancing at Talia, I tell her that I'll only be a minute and that if anything came up to have the nurse practitioner cover it until I return.

I shouldn't be so surprised that he's here, but I am. For some reason, I thought it would have been sooner than this though.

I follow Peter outside, he holds the door open with a smile as I step through.

I nearly choke on a laugh that threatens to escape, he never did any of this shit when we were together.

Turning to face him, I run my eyes over him and wonder what I ever saw in him to begin with. His hair is slightly longer than usual, but other than that he looks exactly the same as the last time I saw him. I'm not sure why it took me so long to realize that nothing good would ever come from this relationship, and I'm ashamed that I can't even figure out why the hell I stayed with him as long as I did.

"What do you need, Peter? I have clients I need to get too." Trying to speed this little talk up is about like walking a fucking turtle.

"I want you back," he says matter of factly.

Those are the only words he says, and he smiles at me as if it might actually be a possibility for him. I'm silent for a second, waiting for him to tell me all the ways he's planning on changing in order to make this relationship work, but he's silent. He doesn't say anything else, just stares at me with that stupid ass smile on his smug face.

I scoff. "Are you serious?"

He frowns, narrowing his eyes at me. "What do you mean?"

"That's all you're going to say?"

"Well, what else do you expect me to fucking say? I want to get back together, and you know you want to."

I shake my head in disbelief. He clearly doesn't know me at all. The worst part about what he's just said, is that he actually believes it all. He believes that I want to get back together with him, that I'd actually act like nothing ever went wrong between us and just welcome him back with open arms.

"Um, no." I shake my head slightly, crossing my arms over my chest.

"What do you mean no?" His tone changes, and with it comes my full attention. He's getting angry.

"I mean *no*. I'm happy, and I've moved on. It wasn't working with us, and hasn't for years. I'm tired of living the way we were. I love you, Peter, because we were together for so long... but I'm not *in love* with you," I try to explain, I can tell as soon as the word love leaves my lips it's all he's focused on.

"See," he points at me. "You said it yourself that you love me."

My god. I slap a hand to my forehead.

"You didn't listen to me, Peter." I demand. "This is how it always goes, you only hear what you want to hear and nothing more." My voice raises in frustration. It's exhausting dealing with him. And I don't have to deal with him anymore, so why the hell am I even out here arguing? I've had enough, I just need to explain one last thing and hope it's clear. "We are through, I've moved on and we're not getting back together."

He doesn't say anything, so I take a step toward the entrance of my clinic when he grabs ahold of my arm and jerks me around to face him. He's holding my arm tight, and this is something I'm not used to from him. Peter is normally a very distant person, at least in the last few years he has been, but I've never witnessed him being so aggressive.

I grab his arm, remembering the self-defense classes I used to take with Nicole when we were in college and shove his hand one way while I pull the hand he's using to hold mine in the other. It breaks his hold, only for a moment, which is when my brain registers that I need to get the fuck out of here. Just before he moves to grab me again, a loud voice cuts through the air and Peter is shoved away from me.

"Back the fuck up." Declan's in front of me, and the tone in his voice is unlike anything I've ever heard before. His hands are fisted at his side, and he looks ready to lunge at any second. I step forward, resting a hand on his back while grabbing one of his hands with my own. His fingers uncoil from the ball he'd formed, tangling with mine. I don't miss the look on Peter's face when he notices the movement. Declan's eyes never move from Peter's. "You need to go."

"You do—"

I interrupt him, taking a step to stand between them but Declan's arm darts out, halting me from going any further. "You need to leave, Peter. I've told you, I don't know how many times that you and I are through. This is goodbye."

He doesn't move right away, he just stares at me with his eyes bouncing to Declan's hand and back to my eyes. Finally, when he realizes that Declan isn't going to back down and there's no point in a fight, he turns and heads down the sidewalk toward his car, shaking his head the entire time.

I doubt I'll be hearing from him anymore after this. Peter isn't stupid, and he knows this is a fight he won't win. He's heard the stories of Declan from high school, and I think he's probably always known that he was competing with a man from my past. This is goodbye for the two of us, and he knows it.

Declan doesn't move, he watches Peter's every move until he's pulling out of the parking lot and onto the main road. Once his car disappears, he turns to me, his eyes searching my face for any emotion.

"Are you okay?" he asks, pulling me to him, he pushes the sleeve of my white coat up so he can look at my elbow. It's slightly red, nothing major but his eyes flash again and

I know he wants to kill Peter right now for putting his hands on me.

"Yeah, sorry about that."

He shakes his head. "He the ex?"

I nod.

"Fucking tool."

I swat at his stomach, causing us both to laugh.

"What are you doing here?" I ask, pushing the incident that just took place from my mind.

"Rescuing you." He smirks.

"I don't need rescuing," I remind him, rubbing at the spot on my arm where Peter grabbed me.

"I know that, but I enjoy doing it." His fingers lace behind my back, bringing me closer to him while I link mine around his neck. "I just wanted to see you, I know you were busy last night but I meant what I said."

The words from his letter flash in my head, making me smile.

"We need to take this slow..." I breathe. "I still have a lot of fear about the past and it repeating itself again," I explain.

My heart wants to throw me over the cliff right into those old emotions that are swirling from the past, but my head is trying to be logical and remind myself of what happened. History often repeats itself, and Declan and I hardly know each other anymore. It's been years since we've been together, a lot has changed.

"I know, baby. And I'll give you all the time you need." He leans down pressing his lips softly to my nose.

I can't fight away the butterflies that erupt in my tummy, even if I wanted to.

22

DECLAN

THE ANGER that circulated through my veins when I saw his hand on my girl is unlike anything I've ever felt before. She thinks I don't notice the way she's rubbing her arm from where he touched her, but I notice everything about her.

"So, is Peter going to be a problem?" I ask, searching her eyes for the answer. She pulls away, but isn't more than a step from me.

I haven't dated anyone since Lou, I haven't had an interest in anyone. Every time I was with another woman, it was just sex... but there was only one person I ever pictured during those moments and she's standing in front of me right now.

"No, and if he is, I'll handle it." Her hand moves to her arm again. "We haven't been officially split up for long, but our relationship was over long before that time." She looks at the ground, kicking at a rock on the concrete with her sneaker. "I suspected that he was cheating on me, but I can't be sure and never found proof." She shrugs her shoulders as if it's not a big deal.

Her thoughts on this dude only fuel the anger I felt moments ago, and now all I want to do is rip this motherfucker's head off even more.

"I'm sorry, baby." I shake my head, wrapping my arms around her again.

"Why are you sorry?"

"Because, I feel like it's my fault. If I hadn't been such a fuckup in the past, you wouldn't be in this position right now," I admit.

That guilt alone could eat a man alive.

"What happened with Peter and me is not your fault." She rises to her toes and presses her lips against mine. It's soft, warm, and exactly what I need to calm my racing heart. "And we're not talking about the past right now."

"Okay," I mumble before her lips are on me again. I break the kiss and pull her against my chest, burying my face in her neck. She smells like peaches today, and it's so intoxicating and such a fucking turn on. I'm getting a boner in the middle of the fucking sidewalk, just hugging my girl. "So, we're taking this slow," I repeat her words from earlier, she nods against me before I pull away to look at her face. "You set the pace, okay? Because I'd fucking marry you tomorrow if I could." I don't even realize what I've said until her eyes widen.

She recovers quickly though, a small smirk appearing on those perfect lips.

"Slower than that." She giggles, bringing my lips to hers again. "Much slower than that."

"Alright," I agree, and my world feels like it's finally

righting again. Like its back on it's axis and I can breathe a little easier.

"I need to get back to work, but call me later?" She smiles, and it fucking hits me in the chest.

"Yeah, baby. Have a good day." I kiss her again before watching as she walks inside.

I smile, shaking my head at the turn of events that I wasn't fucking expecting. When my mom asked where I'd been when I didn't come home the other night, I thought she might explode with excitement when I told her who I was with.

Never in my life did I think my mom would scream with joy when I told her I was out all night with a girl. But Lou's the exception to that, clearly.

She went on and on, asking a million questions about what happened and telling me I better not screw it up this time because she wants a daughter-in-law and it better be Lou.

Little does she know, I plan to make that happen eventually, just after this *slow* stage wears off. The only problem, is figuring out what the fuck I'm going to do with my career.

Heading back toward my truck, my phone vibrates in my pocket. No one ever calls me, it's usually just text messages. The name on the screen has dread pooling in my stomach as I slide my thumb across the screen to answer it.

"Sir," I say, exhaling a breath I didn't realize I was holding in.

"Sargeant." His voice is deep, and I know what's to come. "Have you made your decision?"

"No, sir. Not yet."

"Listen, Sanchez. We've known each other a long time now."

I nod, even though he can't see me.

"Your country is grateful for your service this far, but we're not done. There's rumors circulating that we may be deploying to the Middle East, and I want you to command our men into victory."

"I understand, sir." And I do, I know my place in the military world. To be honest, when I came home, it was only meant to be a break. One that was going to get my head on straight, but then my mom started expressing her concerns, and now I have Lou back. Or at least I hope I have her back. Things are different now, and re-enlisting isn't going to be as easy.

My dad's no longer a deciding factor, I lost that feeling of closeness to my dad when I was shipped out for my second tour and nearly didn't make it. I haven't told anyone about what happened then, not my mom, not a soul, aside from the therapist they are paying to fix my fucked up shit. The only ones who understand are the ones that were with me on the deployment.

War is cold, and lonely.

But I've done it twice now, and what do I have to show for any of it? Nothing, nothing worth meaning anyways. I'm proud to serve my country, and I don't regret enlisting when I did... I just regret enlisting the way I did.

"How are your sessions with Dr. Tinnin?"

"They're good, sir."

"Good. Keep doing what you have to do in order to get back here." He ends the call without saying another word.

The weight of that call is already growing, pushing

down on me and making it harder to breathe. How the fuck am I going to tell Lou about my deployment?

My phone vibrates in my hand again, this time alerting me of a text message.

Nick: When are you coming back man?

Me: Not sure yet.

Nick: Don't leave me hanging, bro.

The guilt weighs heavy. Nick and I enlisted at the same time, went through bootcamp together before Marine Combat Training, and we've just been lucky enough to be together the rest of the time. We work well together, so I don't know if that has something to do with them grouping us together each time. But what I do know is that there isn't a better group of men to fight for our country than the ones I'm blessed to walk alongside each day.

Me: I won't, Nick. I've just got some stuff going on here.

Nick: Did you win her back?

I smile to myself, he's known about Lou from the very beginning. If I would have listened to him years ago, I'd have already been back here and fighting for her. Which probably would have been a shit show, considering she was dating Peter.

Me: Working on it.

Nick: Good luck, my man.

Me: I'll need it.

Nick: Keep me posted. Rumors going around about a deployment, not much else has been said though. At least not anything I've heard that seems enough to bring us in.

Shit..

Me: Damn, bro.

Nick: It fucking sucks without you here though.
Me: No doubt.
Nick: Holler at me later.

I don't respond, I just slide my phone back into my pocket and head for my truck. The only thing I need right now is a run and I'm sure Gunnar would be on board with that too.

23

LOU

IT'S BEEN a few days since Declan and I decided to take things slow. Every time I start to get excited about what's happening between us, that fear of what if creeps back into my mind.

Slowly spiraling until I'm doubting the entire thing.

"Lou," my mother says my name, snapping me out of my thoughts. "Aren't you going to eat? You've barely touched your food."

I laugh, unable to hold it in because she sounds just like she did when I was in high school.

"Yeah, sorry. My mind is kind of all over the place," I admit, I haven't told anyone about Declan and I yet, aside from Nicole.

"Oh?" She takes a bite of her salad, waiting for me to give her more info on why I'm so scatterbrained.

"Declan's back." I take my first bite, watching her reaction.

"I know." She smirks.

Of course she does, nothing happens in this town

without my mother hearing about it from someone. "I also heard that you two put on quite a show in front of your clinic the other day." She takes another bite. "Along with Peter."

"Who told you that?" I ask, knowing she won't tell me. She never does.

"I will never reveal my sources." She chuckles, waving her fork in my direction. The sound makes me smile. "Is this when you're going to tell me that the two of you are back together?"

"Mom," I warn.

"What? I've always liked the boy. I didn't agree with how he handled things between the two of you back then, but I understood his need to enlist."

"What?" I ask, dropping my fork to my plate. "What do you mean?"

"Oh, honey. You were so heartbroken when he left, but I saw the way he was with you. You didn't move without him following along, that boy was in love with you then and I have no doubt that those feelings didn't fade when the years passed. He had just lost his father, a decorated war veteran, so of course he joined the military." She says it as if it was plain to see.

"I–"

"Don't," She smiles. "Don't say anything, you were young." She shrugs her shoulders. "The only thing that matters is now, and the two of you are getting a second chance. That's what really matters. Second chances don't happen every day." She lifts her glass to her lips, taking a drink. Her words repeat in my head, *Second chances don't happen every day.* "Are you bringing him to the vow renewal?"

"I haven't really thought about it. I didn't want to have any drama on your big day." I look at Tessa who nearly chokes on her water.

"Yeah, I'm sure your brother will be thrilled to have Declan there." She smiles. "But, if he makes you happy, then I'm happy and I promise your brother won't be an issue."

"Or he'll have to answer to his mother, and we all know how he feels about that." My mom laughs, brushing a piece of hair from her eyes.

"I'll ask him, I don't even know if he'll feel comfortable going or not," I admit, there is a lot of bad blood between Kyle and him, and I don't want to ruin my parents' renewal.

We finish eating lunch, chatting about a few things that need to be finished before the renewal. Once we're done, I drive my mom home before heading home.

It's quiet when I walk in, almost too quiet.

Maybe I should get a dog or something. I remember what my mom said about inviting Declan to the renewal. Grabbing my phone, I choose to send a text, unsure of where he's at or if he's busy right now.

Me: Hey, have a question for you! If you're not busy.

I take a deep breath and slowly blow it out. I'm so damn nervous, and I don't know why. It's almost comical, I'm never like this.

Declan: Hit me.

That was a fast response. I smile to myself.

Me: So... My parents are having a vow renewal ceremony.

Declan: Yeah?

Me: And, I was wondering if you'd want to go with me.

He doesn't respond right away, but it shows that he's read my text. Shit, what if this was too soon? And I'm the one that kept saying I wanted to take things slow and here I am asking him to a big family function.

Me: You don't have to, I mean... it was just a thought. My mom suggested it, and I don't really want to go with anyone else.

Declan: Lol. Sorry, I was letting my dog out. I'd like to go with you, if you think it's okay.

Me: You have a dog?

How did I not know he had a dog?

Declan: Yeah. Gunnar, he's a German Shepard.

Me: Can't wait to meet him.

Declan: How about tonight? Mom's cooking, come for dinner.

Me: Are you sure? She won't mind?

I bite my bottom lip. I've not talked to his mom in a while. After he left, I avoided her like the plague but that was short lived because I ran into her at the diner one day. I should have known better than to think that she'd be upset with me, but even knowing that, it was hard to see her because she reminded me so much of him.

Declan: Are you kidding me? My mom loves you... probably more than me.

Me: Yeah, you're right... Okay, what time?

Declan: Six too late?

Me: Six is perfect.

I grab a water from my fridge and collapse onto my couch. I'm going to Declan's for dinner, and suddenly I'm so nervous that I find myself checking the clock, waiting with every tick until it's time to get ready.

———

PULLING into his mother's house is kind of surreal, to think that after all these years I'm back here. Getting ready to have dinner with her like we used to, it's just an odd feeling but one that brings a smile to my face.

Before I even have the car in park, I see the front door of their modest home opening with a smiling Declan stepping out. I shove my car door open and climb out, expecting to be greeted by Declan, but I'm stunned when a large German Shepherd barrels through the front door, heading toward me.

Oh shit. My eyes widen in realization that he isn't slowing down the closer he gets. His paws hit a mud puddle as he gallops through it on his trek to me.

I'm wearing a cream colored sweater, he has mud covering his paws. This is not happening...

I hear Declan call his name, but either the dog is too excited he isn't registering his words or he just doesn't care. In the next instance, he jumps and I'm slammed to the gravel drive onto my back from the force of the contact. His dog licks the side of my face and the strength of his tail wagging has him shaking side to side. I run my hand through his fur, scratching behind his ears and laugh as I turn my head to get away from his licking.

"Shit." Declan is by my side, pulling his dog off of me by the collar before lifting me to my feet.

I laugh, because... could this shit be any more fucked up right now? I mean really?

Looking down at my shirt, I realize my cream sweater is now more of a tie dye brown with several paw prints across my midriff. Damn, this dog has huge paws.

"C'mon," He tips his head in the direction of his home. "You can borrow some of my clothes." He smiles down at me, enjoying the fact that I'll have to wear his clothes for the remainder of the evening.

"What a great first impression..." I trail off, looking down at my shirt.

Declan grabs my hand, pulling me along behind him as we head towards the front door. "You've already met my mom." He laughs.

"I know, but this feels like a big deal." I stop, pulling on his hand to face me. I've been here more times than I can count, but this time is different. It's a huge fucking deal, and signifies the next step in this relationship that we're rekindling.

"I know, baby." He takes my face in his hands, rubbing his nose across mine before softly covering my mouth with his. That one simple touch takes all the nerves that are rising away. "C'mon." He kisses my forehead and turns back for the front door.

He holds the door open for me, allowing me to step through and I'm hit with the smell of his mother's cooking causing my stomach to growl. Nothing about the inside of the house has changed, the same blanket is folded neatly on the back of the couch, the same one we'd cuddle under when we were watching movies late at night. The memories hit me hard, and I have to blink several times to keep the tears from coming to the surface.

"Lou!" His mom squeals with excitement when she sees me. "Oh, how I've missed you."

She crosses the room, wrapping me in a hug and not caring a bit about the mud that's drying on my sweater.

"Mrs. Sanchez." I hug her bag, fighting back the emotions clogging my throat once again.

She pulls me back to look at me, her eyes roam over my torso down to my feet. "You're too thin, I'll feed you." She smiles, and I smile too. You can't not smile at his mother and her need to take care of everyone around her. "I see you've met Gunnar." She laughs, gesturing to my poor sweater.

"Yeah, he greeted her alright." Declan laughs, stepping up behind me and resting his hands on my shoulder.

I turn my head slightly, looking up at him and the smile he flashes me takes my breath away. His mother looks from him to his hands before a smile breaks out across her face.

"I'm gonna get her some clothes."

"Okay, hurry up. Dinner is almost ready, and I have a BINGO date with your aunt tonight." Her mouth tilts at the end, making me wonder what's going on here.

He pulls me down the hall toward his bedroom, pushing the door open and allowing me to walk through. The smell hits me first, it smells just like him. He moves to his dresser and shuffles through it until he finds me something to wear. He pulls out a green t-shirt with the Marine logo across the back. He shoves one drawer shut before pulling open another for a pair of gray sweatpants.

"Here." He hands them to me. "I'm going to go rinse Gunnar's paws off so we can make sure we don't have a repeat of what just happened." He laughs, kissing my temple before walking out of the room.

Once the door shuts, I take a minute to look around, letting my eyes roam over every inch of his room. His bed is in the same spot as it was back then, the only difference now is the blanket across the foot of it with paw prints printed on it, which I'm assuming belongs to Gunnar.

Moving to his desk, I run my hand over the back of his chair, scanning everything on the surface. My breath hitches when I see a picture of me from high school. Why did he keep this?

I don't know how long I stare at the picture before the door to his room opens again and he steps in. He looks at me, frowning when he sees I've still not changed from my muddy clothes.

"You okay?" He steps closer to me, his eyes boring into mine. "What's wrong?"

I point at the picture, watching as his eyes follow my hand and realization sets in.

"Why do you still have this?" My eyes move from him to the picture, remembering the day it was taken. It was so long ago, but it honestly feels like it was yesterday.

"I've not been back home in a few years." He admits, and for some reason that shocks the hell out of me. "I was too scared to run into you if I did, I wasn't ready."

"Supper!" his mom shouts down the hall, reminding us both that we need to get back out there.

"I need to change."

He doesn't make a move to leave so I start pulling my shirt over my head, and watch as his eyes darken with need. I slowly start unbuttoning my jeans and slide them down my legs before grabbing the sweats from the bed. I have to roll them three times to fit my length, but when I pull his Marine shirt over my head, I can see him shaking from holding back but I'm honestly impressed with his strength.

"You're so fucking perfect, you know that right?"

I don't say anything, and neither does he because his moms yelling down the hall for us again.

"We're coming!" he yells back, turning his attention back to me. "To be continued."

Dinner is delicious, just like I knew it would be. His mother plates our food, sitting it in front of us before making her own and having a seat. No matter how many times I offered to help her so she could sit down quicker, she refused.

"Lou," Mrs. Sanchez takes a drink of her water. "How is your clinic going? I was so sad to see Dr. Millings retire, he delivered Declan." She looks over at him and smiles.

"It's going really good." I smile. "I never thought I'd have my own clinic, especially not this early in my career."

"I hear good things though, dear." She reaches across the table and pats my hand. Declan looks at me, something that looks a lot like pride fills his eyes.

Conversation flows easily, and I feel as if there was never a time distance between us. I've nearly cleared my plate when Declan stands to fill his again. That obviously hasn't changed.

"So, are the two of you back together?" Mrs. Sanchez asks, her eyes bouncing from me to Declan as he returns to his seat.

"Momma," he whines.

"What?" She shrugs. "A mother just needs to know these things."

"Mom."

"What? It's not like I'm asking if you're being careful in the bed." She laughs at the look on Declan's face. "Not that I expect you to, I'm not getting any younger you know."

It's me that nearly chokes this time. On my water. I was not expecting her to say that. Nope, that one shocked me.

Declan groans, throwing his head back as he looks at the ceiling. I'm nearly coughing up a lung, convinced that this water is going to kill me.

How sad... death by choking on water.

"Oh, stop it." Mrs. Sanchez waves her hand at Declan. "I'm just saying..." She shrugs again in a playful manner. "I'm sure your mother would want another grandbaby."

That makes me laugh. "I'm sure she would."

Declan slowly lowers his chin, looking over at me with a fire in his eyes. One that lets me know what his plans are for the rest of the night.

After dinner, his mom heads out for her BINGO game while we take Gunnar on a walk around his neighborhood. The night air paired with the warmth of Declan's body pressed against mine as we reminisce about the past is slowly taking away some of the fears I have been harboring since we've rekindled our relationship.

"So, my mom won't be home for a while." He smiles down at me, pulling me tighter against him. "If she comes home at all."

"What do you mean?"

"Sometimes they play BINGO so late that she stays at my aunt's place." He chuckles.

"Seriously? BINGO gets that serious?" I chuckle, thinking of all the little old ladies that play and their collection of colored dabbers.

"You have no idea." He shakes his head, his shoulders shaking with laughter. "But, that means we have the house to ourselves."

And just like that, the heat between my legs makes me

clench them together just from the husky tone in his voice. Instead of finishing the walk, we turn and double back the way we came to get to his mom's house quicker. This time our slow walk has turned into an almost jog.

As soon as we reach the door, Declan's hands are on my waist and he's pushing me down the hall toward his room. He didn't even bother taking the leash off of Gunnar when we walked in, he slung it in the direction Gunnar was going and kicked the front door shut with his boot.

I'm pushed against his closed door, his hands moving to grab my ass before he lifts me effortlessly into his arms. My legs wrap around his waist and my center grinds down on his erection. Reaching behind me, I twist the knob of the door without thinking and both of us fall to the floor. Laughter is the only sound in the room as Declan leans back to make sure I'm okay.

"Holy shit, are you hurt?" He looks at me with concern in his eyes.

"I'm fine," I say between laughs. "I didn't think that one through."

"No," He shakes his head. "No, you didn't."

My hand runs over his chest, stopping against his abs as my finger trails his rippled muscles through his shirt. His eyes raise to mine again, and this time there's something brewing within them. Something I recognize all too well, and can feel deep in my gut.

Longing.

More than just this moment, it's a longing for what we've lost over the past. The life we could have had together, the life we were supposed to have together.

"You're so goddamn beautiful." His hand reaches out,

sweeping across my cheek. The feeling brings a tingle to my skin, and I commit this moment to memory.

His touch moves farther until his hand is wrapped around the back of my neck, lifting my head closer to him as he leans forward. He paralyzes me with his piercing blue eyes, his eyes close with his lips hovering just an inch away from mine.

"I love you," he whispers, just before he slams his mouth into mine. His lips are full, his kiss deep, portraying all the emotions that are circling between us right now.

I kiss him back, and it's a kiss unlike any that we've shared before. I'm unable to respond to his words, his hands are moving between us and pulling at his sweats that cover my lower body. He shifts to the side, helping me pull them from my feet before he throws them in the corner of the room and stands.

I'm laying on the floor, just inside his bedroom door with nothing but his t-shirt on and my underwear. His eyes flash as he drinks me in before lifting to tug his shirt over his head. The sight of him makes my mouth water, and this is one of those moments where I'm so fucking thankful for the Marines and what it's done for his body.

His jeans are next, undoing his belt before pulling it free and snapping open the button of his jeans. I swear, when he pulls the zipper down the sound is magnified by the tension between us. I think he's about to pull his boxers down when he pauses and reaches a hand out for me.

I take it, and slowly let him pull me from the plush carpet. He lifts me once again, kicking the door closed before walking toward the bed. He doesn't release me, not until I'm in the center of his bed and frozen from his eyes.

He smirks, moving his hands back to his boxers and slowly peels them down his muscled thighs until he's standing in front of me without an inch of fabric covering him. His dick stands at attention, begging to be touched, and just when I'm about to lean up and reach for him, he pushes me back to the bed, dropping his lips to my ear. "This is all about you, baby."

A moan leaves me, causing him to chuckle as he slides my shirt up my body and over my head. My bra and underwear aren't anything special, but the look in his eyes right now tells me that he doesn't give a shit what I'm wearing. I arch my back, giving him access to unsnap my bra. He slowly pulls the straps down my body, bringing a trail of chill bumps in its path. My underwear is torn at the sides, pulling a gasp from my lips at the sensation.

Declan looks down at me, smirking again. That fucking smirk could send me over the edge right now, but when his head dips and the feel of his tongue slides through my lips... his smirk is all but forgotten. He teases me, moving his tongue against me so that I'm clenching the sheets beneath me before he pulls away, leaving me breathless and frustrated.

He moves again, and I think he's about to continue what he started but the feeling of his dick at my entrance has my eyes snapping to his before he leans over my body and kisses me hard.

"You're mine," he whispers. "Say it."

"I'm yours."

"Always?" he demands the answer, but little does he know I've always been his.

"Always." I bite my bottom lip as he pushes all the way

into me in one long, slow thrust. His eyes never leave mine as our moans mix in the air around us.

"You're so fucking soft." He grinds his hips into mine, moaning in the process while I lift my hips, willing him deeper.

Once again, he stops, pulling out and leaving me frustrated from his absence. He flips us, sits up, and pulls me onto his lap. His hands slide down my thighs as I line myself up with him and sink down until he's filling me once again. He's deeper this way, and a shiver breaks out over my skin, bringing that same sexy smirk to his lips once again.

I roll my hips, letting myself get lost in the feel of him. This is what it was always like between us, the connection deeper than just sex. His hand slowly slides up my side, taking one of my breasts into his hand. He runs a thumb over my nipple, toying with me until I lose my stride and grab the back of his neck and bring his mouth to my bud. His tongue swirls, bringing out a sensation that sends me to my peak as I continue moving against him.

"I'm so close..." I cry out. He thrusts into me, pushing deeper and deeper each time until my head falls back onto my shoulders. Our bodies are slick with sweat, but that doesn't stop our movements.

He reaches up, grabbing my hair and tugging it slightly to make my toes curl as he drives into me. He flexes inside of me, and my pussy squeezes him back bringing a sound from his lips that causes me to spiral into the bliss of please.

I pull his face into my hands, kissing him to hide my moans of pleasure. His grunts are hidden as he thrusts into me harder, and takes my ass in his palms. I feel the swell of his cock before he thrusts one last time and pulls me tightly against his body.

Both of us are breathless, but there's a smile on my face when I remember the words he said to me before. Rolling off of him, I maneuver myself so that I'm laying against his chest staring at the ceiling above us as the fan slowly spins, not giving near enough air to cool our overworked bodies.

I'm lost in the scent around me, and the emotions barreling through me.

"You okay?" He turns his head to look down at me.

"I love you, too."

He smiles, pulling me tighter against him as I shut my eyes and just feel this moment together.

24

DECLAN

Lou left early this morning, not wanting to chance a run in with my mom. Even though I'm a grown ass man, and I'm pretty sure Mom knew what was going to happen when she decided to stay at my aunt's house last night.

My mind has covered every second that happened last night, ending in her saying those three words I've been dying to hear for fifteen years. At that moment, I thought I was on top of the motherfucking world. A feeling I haven't had since we were together last.

The smell of sausage floats down the hall, and I know my mom has made it home. Throwing my legs over the edge of the bed, I stand and stretch before pulling a pair of shorts from my drawer and sliding them on. When I look back at my bed, I can't hide the smile that breaks across my face at the thought of how she looked tangled in my sheets.

Once I reach the kitchen, my mom turns with a skillet in her hand and walks toward the table.

"Did you two have a good evening?" She giggles and for

some reason I feel like a teenage boy who broke all the rules my mother set out for me.

"Yeah," I say, choking on the lie when my mother cuts her eyes at me.

"Good." She sets the skillet on the center of the table before she begins dishing food onto a plate for me. I wait until she's finished to take my first bite. "I'm glad the two of you are working on things."

"Me, too." I laugh, remembering the conversation we had at dinner, shaking my head as I chew my bite. "I love her."

"Oh, I know you do, sweet boy. And she loves you, otherwise she wouldn't have come here yesterday." She reaches over, resting her palm against my cheek as she stares at me. "The two of you were always meant to be together."

"You think so?" I look down at my plate but pull my eyes back to her when she jerks my chin.

"I know so."

Once breakfast is done, I clean up and take a quick shower before my next session with Dr. Tinnin. I plan on heading to the gym when I'm done with that. Although, I could probably skip a day after the workout I got last night.

Flipping open the laptop on my desk, I look up at her picture on the wall as I sit in my chair and log into the meeting window that Dr. Tinnin likes to use. After a few minutes, his face fills the screen.

"Declan, good morning," he says, lifting his coffee mug to his lips. "Excuse my coffee, I'm lagging this morning."

"No worries." I smile.

"You seem to be in a good mood, anything you'd like to share?" He chuckles, writing in that damn notebook of his.

"I think Lou and I are, uh," I trail off, trying to figure out the best way to explain it. "I think we're back together."

"Ah, that's good news."

"Yeah, yeah it is." I run a hand over my face, trying to hide my smile.

"How will you deal with leaving her when you come back to base?" It's like I'm hit in the face with a bucket of ice water when he says those words.

"I haven't really thought about that."

"Yeah? Have you thought about what you might say to her?"

I shake my head.

"What have you told her about your career?"

"Well, I mean I've told her about why I left before and how I didn't want her to wait around on me like my mom always did when my dad left."

He nods, gesturing for me to continue.

"But, she doesn't know why I'm here now, really."

"What does she think?"

I shrug. "I'm not sure, we haven't talked about it."

"You haven't talked to her about your struggles? What about your lack of sleep from time to time or the nightmares?"

"No, I don't want to burden her with that."

"Declan, have you thought about going to see Abigail?"

I lean back in my chair, turning my attention to the picture of Lou on the wall.

"I wouldn't even know what to say. Or where she lives."

"I think you'd benefit from checking in with her, I can forward you her contact information if you'd like."

I nod, unsure if I want to contact her or not.

"You're the doc."

"You're shutting down, why?"

"What do you mean?" I ask.

"You're defensive now. The mention of Abigail and your mood completely changed. You were talking openly about Lou, but once Abigail was brought up, you began to shut down."

"Whatever you say." I shrug, I know I'm being an ass, but I don't care.

"Don't allow what you're rekindling with Lou to cover up your trauma with Maurene and Abigail, otherwise you're dooming your relationship from the start." Dr. Tinnin writes in his book, waiting for me to respond.

"You don't fucking know what you're talking about," I bark.

"Just think about what I've said, Declan. If you love Lou, the way I think you do, then you need to have this conversation with her and be completely open."

Fuck.

The session ends with him reminding me, like always, that my time here is limited and it was meant for me to overcome the obstacles that continue to haunt me. I thought I was doing a damn good job of that until he pointed out that I could possibly be covering up my issues with Lou.

I stand, grabbing my gym bag and my phone. I need to tell her, I know that. She's been completely open with me, and I need to do the same.

Me: *I'm heading to the gym. Let's do dinner tonight, I'll pick you up at seven.*

I pocket my phone and don't pull it out again until I get to the gym.

Lou: *Okay, babe. Can't wait.* She attaches an emoji blowing a heart.

I smile as I walk in the door, looking down at the text I just received from Lou. I don't know how I'll explain all of this to her, or what she'll even think of me after I do. Either way, it needs to be said. And as much as I don't want to admit to Dr. Tinnin being right, I think maybe this will help me in the long run.

Moving toward the back of the gym, I walk into the locker room and set my bag on the bench in the center of the room before unlocking the locker that I've paid for.

I'm tying my shoes when I hear someone enter the locker room. I don't look up but hear the "Motherfucker" and know exactly who it is.

"What the fuck are you doing here?" Kyle drops his bag to the floor, his fingers curl into fists at his side. "You need to leave."

Is he fucking serious?

"I'm not leaving." I stand, placing my foot that was just on the bench to the floor.

Kyle and I are about the same size, and now we're built about the same as well.

"I'm not talking about the fucking gym." He comes a step closer. "I'm talking about this fucking town. You never should have come back here. You're just going to fuck her over again."

That has me stepping closer now. "You don't have any idea what you're talking about."

"The fuck I don't." He's in my face. "Who do you think was there every goddamn time she cried over your sorry ass? Who do you think was the one forcing her to eat so she wouldn't starve to death?"

What? My eyes widen at his words, the pain aching in my chest all over again.

"It was me, so as far as I'm concerned, you're no fucking good for her and need to get the hell out of here." He points in the direction of the door.

"I'm not leaving, Kyle. You can fucking deal with me." I shove my bag in the locker before slamming it shut. "And that's for your sister to decide. But I'm not fucking going anywhere." I look back at my locker as I hook the lock back in place. When I turn my head, I feel his fist slam against my jaw.

Mother fucker.

I swing without thinking, taking him to the ground in the process. Straddling his hips, I hit him again before pinning his hands to his sides and staring at him. "I never wanted to leave her." His eyes widen. "I never wanted to fucking leave her but I had to. I loved her, I still do. The last thing I wanted was to hurt her, but I knew if she'd have went with me, it would have ruined her life and I couldn't fucking do that."

His shifts beneath me, so I release his arms and push off of him. Running a hand through my hair, I squeeze my eyes shut tightly, remembering the pain I felt from walking away from her that day.

"My dad had just died. The one person in my life that I looked up to more than anyone, and he was just gone. I never got to say goodbye, I never got to tell him that I was planning to marry Lou, none of that. He was just gone." I choke on the words, turning to look at Kyle. He slowly raises from the spot I had him in on the ground, resting his elbows on his knees as he listens to me. "I watched my mom, every fucking time he walked out the door. I watched her die a little inside from the fear of him never returning." I shake my head and walk toward the far wall, turning to lean against it. "I couldn't fucking do that to your sister. I thought I was making the best choice for her."

"Why didn't you just say all of this?" he asks.

I shake my head, unsure of why I chose the route I did. "I was fucking young, I didn't know what I was doing and I think part of me knew she wouldn't budge. She would have given up all her dreams to come with me, and I didn't feel like I was in the state of mind to fight her on it then. It was the only option that made sense at the time." I kick off the wall, walking closer to him. "I fucking love her, I never stopped."

"I didn't know," he tells me.

"No one did... not even Lou until a little bit ago," I explain.

"And she's okay with it?"

I nod, as far as I know she is. We've talked some, but she knows why I did what I did now and that's enough for me. We can move forward from it all now.

"Shit." He rubs his hand across his brow, dabbing at the cut caused from my hit. "Where'd you learn to fight like that?"

"I'm a Marine." I shrug.

He moves to stand, dusting off his gym shorts as he does it. "If you fucking hurt her, I'll end you. I don't give a fuck what your reasoning is this time, I will end you."

"Understood." If I hurt her again, I'll fucking let him end me.

My phone rings from inside my locker, so I walk toward it while Kyle heads to the bathroom just off the side of the locker room. Pulling the lock free and opening the door, I dig through my things until I find my phone. The name on the screen brings a smile so fucking big to my lips, I feel like my face might actually crack.

My smile never fades as I bring it to my ear and answer, "Hey, babe."

"Hey, I know you're at the gym but real quick..." I can hear her shuffling around and it makes me smile harder. "What should I wear tonight?"

"Whatever you want. You'll be gorgeous in anything. I know that."

"Stop it." She giggles. "God, I sound like a high schooler." There's a slight pause. High school isn't the best topic for us still. "Any preferences?"

"Well, if we're talking about preferences, then I'd prefer you naked." I huff out a laugh.

"Okay, you're no help. Go get buff or whatever. See you tonight."

I tell her goodbye before locking my phone back up in my locker and walking into the open gym.

There's a hell of a lot of nervous energy to burn off today.

25

LOU

I've been looking out the window every three seconds, waiting for Declan's truck to pull into the driveway for our date. I was shocked when I got the text that he wanted to go out tonight, but the excitement made that fade quickly.

A few minutes later, a loud roar of an engine has me peeking out the window again. Declan's truck pulls into my driveway, and I watch as he throws open the driver's door and climbs out.

He's dressed in dark wash jeans, and a black button down shirt that hugs his biceps and makes me drool. I'm suddenly thankful I curled my hair today instead of wearing it straight.

Declan knocks once he reaches my front door, and I slowly blow out a deep breath before pulling the door open. His eyes meet mine, but slowly slide south as he takes me in.

"You look fucking incredible." He smiles, stepping over the threshold and pulling me against him.

His mouth covers mine, the taste of mint evades my

senses when his tongue brushes against mine. I press my body against him, holding his hips tightly against mine.

"If we don't stop, we'll never make it to dinner." He pulls away from me. "And I have some stuff I want to talk to you about that is important... but right now you have me rethinking it all."

I laugh, nervously. I have no clue what he could be meaning by things he needs to tell me, so dread pools in my stomach at the idea of him leaving me again.

"Got everything you need?"

I nod, looking down at the purse on my arm. He steps out of the way, letting me walk outside first while he locks and closes the door behind me. He guides me to his truck with his hand on the small of my back. Once I'm situated inside and the buckle is in place, he shuts the door and rounds to his side.

"Where are we going?" I ask as he pulls his truck from my driveway.

"It's a surprise." He winks, looking back at the road.

"Ugh." I groan, leaning my head against the headrest and look out the window.

"Still don't like surprises?" He reaches over, placing his hand on my thigh. My own fingers tangle with his.

"I like them." I shrug. "When I know about them."

"Then it's not a surprise." The sound of his laughter calms my nerves. If it was something bad, he wouldn't be laughing, right?

The drive is quick, and I smile when he pulls into the diner we used to come to when we were teenagers. It was like our date night sanctuary on the weekends. Every Friday night, after a football game, we'd come here.

He'd order us both burgers, and a chocolate shake to share.

"I know it's not a fancy restaurant, but it's us." He shrugs, pushing open his door before coming to mine. I take his hand, dropping my feet to the ground.

He leads me inside, and we're ushered to the booth we used to frequent.

"Did you do this?"

He shrugs. "Maybe."

We sit across from each other, the waitress approaches and just as I expected, or more less hoped, Declan ordered us both burgers and a milkshake to share.

"So, what did you want to talk about?" I ask, ready to get the elephant in the room out in the open.

He sucks in a deep breath, holds it for a moment and then slowly blows it out. "You know I was deployed in the past?"

I nod. I mean I did but I didn't, if that makes sense.

"Well, there was an incident." He moves his hands so that they're close to his face, and I can tell that what he's trying to say right now is something that's difficult for him.

"Babe, you don't have to tell me."

"Yeah, yeah I do. You need to know why I'm home."

I nod, letting him continue.

"There was a hostage situation, I won't go into the details because they'll haunt you forever if I do... but it was a mother and her daughter. The mother didn't make it, but the daughter did. Granted, she's probably fucked up from everything she's endured." He shrugs. "The mom was shot in front of me, and the only thing that I saw was you."

I lean back slightly, not expecting those words to come from his mouth. "What?"

"She looked so much like you, and I panicked. I lost control, I was way out of line and killed the fucker." He shakes his head, looking out of the window next to our table. "It fucked with my head enough that they forced me to take a medically leave, if you will, until I could sort through this shit."

"Oh, Declan." I reach across the table, taking his hand in mine. "I'm so sorry."

He shakes his head. "You've been so good for me, but then my conversation with my therapist this morning had me thinking if I was really making progress or just using our relationship to cover up the shit I'm really needing to work through." He mumbles something but I don't catch what it is before his eyes lock on mine. "You were part of what I needed to work on." He shakes his head again. "I don't want you to think that I'm using you to try to mend this shit in my head."

"I didn't think that at all." And I didn't.

"I'm thinking about going to see Abigail tomorrow morning, that's the daughter."

"I think that's a good idea, Declan. You need closure." I squeeze his hand.

"Yeah?"

"Yeah." I smile.

The rest of our evening is a little lighter, but I can't help but see the emotions that plague him. I guess I was blind to it all before, but now it's like a big red flag and I ache at the thought of him suffering through this for so long.

I hope he finds the peace he's looking for.

26

DECLAN

I BARELY SLEPT LAST NIGHT, all I could think about was seeing Abigail today. Lou was so understanding, and it only reminded me how much I don't deserve her love after everything I've put her through.

"Where are you off to so early?" my mom asks from her chair in the living room as I walk toward the front door.

"I have some things I need to take care of." I vere in her direction and kiss the top of her head. "I don't know what time I'll be back."

"Okay." She has a look of concern etched across her features. "Don't forget the Tucker's are renewing their vows in a few days."

"I know, I won't be too late." I smile, but even she can tell it doesn't reach my eyes.

Walking out to my truck, my stomach is in knots worrying if this is the right decision. If I'm doing the right thing.

What if it only fucks me up more? Or worse, what if it makes Abigail's situation worse?

I climb into my truck and start it up, letting the roar of the engine soothe me. The radio is on, so I reach over and turn it until the volume is down so low I can't hear anything but my own heart beating.

The drive is roughly six hours from my mom's house, I sit in silence the entire ride. My mind goes wild, flashing back to that night of the raid and their rescue... or Abigail's rescue. Picturing Lou's face when Maurene was shot, the ache in my chest grows and nearly takes my breath from my body.

My exit comes into view, the large green sign alerting me that it's time to turn, which means I'm that much closer to Abigail's house. Dr. Tinnin said she's been living with her father since the accident, but he didn't divulge any more information than that.

I check the GPS on my phone, and follow the directions until I'm pulling into the driveway of a small, two story home with red shutters and a matching red door. I suck in a deep breath, holding it for a moment before letting it out through my mouth. My knuckles are nearly white from gripping the steering wheel, and all I want to do is shift my truck into reverse and get the hell out of here.

But then I think of Lou, and I know I have to do this for not only myself but for her too. She deserves the full me, not this broken and pained version.

After another breath, I climb out of my truck and walk up the sidewalk that leads to the front porch. A large, wooden porch swing sways gently with the wind, and I think of how Abigail's mother probably sat there many days and watched her child play. The thought of her never getting to do that again breaks my heart.

I stop in front of the red door, raising my hand to knock but I freeze just before my knuckles hit against the wood.

I can't do this. It's too much.

Turning on my heel, I get to the first step when I hear the door open behind me. I look over my shoulder and see a man, dressed in slacks and a button down opening the door.

"Hi," I say, turning back to face him and hold a hand out to him. "I'm Declan."

"We were wondering when you were going to come by." He smiles, pushing the door open and gesturing for me to come inside. His words calm me, slightly, but I'm still anxious about this entire conversation we're about to have.

I step inside, and my eyes immediately scan the room. It's a small foyer with a living room off to one side, and an office on the other. Straight ahead from where I'm standing is a doorway that leads into the kitchen with a small table sitting next to two large windows that overlook their backyard.

"Let me get Abigail." The man smiles at me. "Please, have a seat." He gestures into the living room before leaving me and walking up the stairs to where I'm guessing Abigail's room is.

I head into the room, toward one of the couches and have a seat. I twiddle my thumbs, trying to work some of the nervous energy out. But it's not really helping. Looking around, I see pictures covering the mantle of the fireplace. A smiling Maurene holds her daughter on Christmas morning in one, and she's tickling her daughter in another. They have a few family pictures, from what looks like different trips they've gone on over the years. In the center of them all, is a picture of Abigail dressed in a leotard while she blows a kiss at the camera.

They had the perfect family, and I wasn't able to save her. I lost her, for them. If I'd have gone in sooner, she might still be alive and Abigail would have her mother, and they'd be adding to these family pictures on the fireplace.

"Mr. Declan?" a small voice says from the door, pulling my eyes from the pictures to her. Abigail stands, her face has healed only leaving emotional scars for now I'm sure.

I stand. "Hi, Abigail."

She walks toward me, and I think she's going to sit in one of the chairs across from the couch, but she surprises me when she keeps coming and wraps her arms around my waist, resting her head against my chest. I'm reluctant at first, completely caught off guard by her action, but eventually my arms wrap around her and hold her close to me.

I never realized how much I needed this, not until now. I'm not normally an emotional guy, I never cry, but I'd be lying to everyone if I said I wasn't fighting the tears that are threatening to fall right now.

Her dad stands in the doorway that separates the living room and the foyer. "I'll give you two a moment." He smiles before turning and heading into the office that's just on the other side.

"Thank you for coming." Abigail pulls away and sits next to me on the couch. "I was wondering if I'd ever get to see you."

"I'm sorry I haven't come sooner," I admit, I didn't know she was waiting on me, or I would have.

"I'm glad you did." She smiles, tucking a strand of her

hair behind her ear. "They said you've been on leave since..." she trails off.

"Yeah, I needed to get my head on straight." I nod.

"Is it?" she asks. "I mean, is everything getting better?"

"Yeah, I think so."

"Me, too." She looks over at the fireplace. "I mean, it's hard every day without my mom here, but it's getting easier with each day."

Her words hit me, and I want to run. I want to climb into my truck and forget that I even came here, but something keeps me rooted in place.

"I'm sorry I couldn't save her."

"But you did? Can't you see that?" She's looking at me with her brows pinched together.

"She didn't make it, Abigail," I tell her, like she doesn't know that her mother died that day.

"I know, but you showed up, and that meant that you were going to save me." I listen to her words but they're not clicking in my brain. "It took me a long time to learn that, and honestly, I'm still struggling but my therapist is good and he helps me see different sides of things. You showed up, and that was enough for my mom. She knew I'd be safe with you."

"Abigail."

"I don't blame you, Declan."

Those four words hit me like a punch in the gut. She doesn't blame me. Abigail doesn't blame me for what happened.

"It's not your fault that those men took us, it's not your fault what happened to us there, it's not your fault that my mother was killed. None of that is your fault."

I shake my head, pulling my eyes away from her.

"You're not to blame, *they* are. You showed up when you were supposed to. You did what *you* were supposed to. I can tell you blame yourself for what happened, but you stopped that man. You killed him that day, and because of your team, I'm here to tell you to stop blaming yourself, Declan. You don't deserve it."

A tear falls from my eyes, my hands resting on my forehead with my elbows against my knees as I look at the maroon and gold rug beneath my feet.

She doesn't blame me.

I feel her hand against my arm, and she slowly pulls it away. When my eyes meet hers, they match my own with tears. "This wasn't your fault, and if you keep blaming yourself for it, I'll never forgive you." She smiles as she says the words, and I know she's trying to lighten the mood.

"Thank you," I choke.

For the first time since that night, I feel the air around me lighten, making it easier to breathe. My shoulders drop, the weight disappearing.

Abigail and I talk a little longer, her father joins us and we talk about the woman Maurene was. They smile and laugh, and tell me all about the pictures on the mantle. When it's time for me to go, I have one thing on my mind.

The only thing I'm ready to do, and that's get back to my girl.

27

DECLAN

When I first started working with Dr. Tinnin I hated it. I didn't think therapy was going to fix the shit that I was dealing with. I can sit here today, staring at the computer screen where Dr. Tinnin sits in his office, writing in that damn notebook of his like he does every session, and say that I feel like a different person than when I first came home.

Dr. Tinnin had a lot to do with that. Now, I don't dread my sessions with him as much as I used to. Granted, they still suck. I still don't like talking about my feelings, but it's been easier to open up more with him during our sessions.

"Well, Declan, I am impressed with your improvement. You've worked through a lot of your problems, mostly the situation that happened with Abigail."

I suck in a breath, hearing her name still brings up the pain, but Dr. Tinnin said that is normal and will be for a while. It was a traumatic experience, but I no longer hold myself responsible for the death of her mother or what happened to her.

"I've been in contact with your Commander, I have cleared you to return to duty."

"Thank you, sir." I pause. "For everything."

"It's been my pleasure, Declan." He tells me that if I ever need anything, I'm always able to contact him.

Once the call ends, I sit and think about where I am now versus when I arrived. Back then, I was certain I didn't deserve anything in life. But now, I have Lou and everything feels right again. Like my world was just put back into orbit.

Gunnar nudges the side of my leg, whining to go outside. "Alright, boy." I scratch between his ears and stand just as my phone buzzes in my pocket.

My hand freezes when I look at the name. I know what this call means. Hesitantly, I swipe my thumb across the screen and slowly bring it to my ear.

"Commander."

"Sanchez, I see you've been cleared for duty."

That was fast.

"Yes, sir."

"Everything tied up on your end?" he asks.

I know what he means, he wants to know where my head is now.

"Yes, sir."

"Good. We have a mission." His voice is stern as he says it. He's probably repeated the same line for the last hour while he's called everyone. I suck in a deep breath.

"How long?"

"You have roughly seventy-two hours," he tells me. "Maybe less."

"I'll be ready," I tell him.

And I will. That's what I do. It's my job. I just don't know how I'm going to tell Lou.

I decided to work outside my mom's house. Getting all those things done I've made a mental note about lately. My time is running out and I need to make sure she's taken care of while I'm gone again.

It's a little chilly, but nothing too terrible that my hoodie doesn't keep me warm. Plus, it's nearly noon so the sun is out and shining, giving me a little extra warmth.

I have a shit ton of work to get finished. One of her gutters is hanging, and the grass is grown across the gravel driveway. If I don't take care of that now, this spring will be even worse to deal with. I need to replace a few pieces of siding, and lucky for us, the local hardware store had a few pieces of her exact siding in stock when I picked it all up yesterday.

Grabbing the ladder from the shed in the backyard, I head back to the front and see Gunner rolling in a pile of leaves that I raked up earlier this morning. He has no care in the world and by the time he's done, I'll have to rake the entire thing again.

As I'm setting the ladder up, extending it so that it'll reach the gutters, I hear a car pulling into the driveway. My hands are still locked on the ladder when I turn my head to see Lou climbing out of the driver's seat of her car.

Fuck she looks gorgeous today.

Her long legs are covered in denim that makes my mouth water, she's wearing a teal puffer jacket that makes her eyes pop even from across the yard. Her hair is pulled into a high ponytail that gives me the perfect look of her long, slender neck.

I'm hard as a rock. Standing in my mother's front yard, all because this girl just climbed out of a damn car.

"Hey." She smiles as she gets closer to where I'm standing.

Thankfully, Gunner is too preoccupied with his leaves to notice her arrival. I laugh to myself, thinking of the last time she was here when Gunner practically pounced on her.

"Hey, babe." I release the ladder and take a step closer to her before wrapping my arms around her waist. Her lips press against mine and the only thought that enters my mind is *home*. She is home for me.

She breaks the kiss, looking from me to the ladder. "What are you doing?"

I release her and walk back toward the ladder. "I'm working on some stuff for mom." I point to the gutters and siding. "It needs to be fixed and replaced."

"Need any help?" she asks, a nervous smile crossing her face.

"Need? Nah."

She looks away.

"Want? Absolutely."

Her eyes slowly shift back to mine. I could get lost in these eyes. Absolutely lost.

"What can I do?"

"Sit there and let me look at ya." I lean forward and kiss her nose.

Gunner takes that moment to realize I'm not the only one in the yard and he darts toward her. This time she's prepared, but no matter how many times I yell his name, he isn't going to listen when she's around.

But I can't blame the boy, nothing would stop me from getting to her either. Not this time.

A few hours later, I have everything fixed except the leaves that Gunner is still jumping around in. Lou tried to rake them up to help contain his mess but he was having no part of it.

"Let's go grab a late lunch," I tell her.

"I'm game, and starved." She holds a hand to her stomach.

"Let me throw him inside, I'll drive." I toss her the keys to my truck so she can get in while I let him in the house and lock up. My mom's been at my aunt's all day, so there is no telling what she's getting into.

Once I get back to my truck, Lou has it started and her seatbelt across her chest. Her head is resting against the headrest and she slowly rolls her head to my side with a lazy smile on her lips.

"When are you gonna let me drive this monster?"

"Monster, huh?" I laugh, shifting the truck into reverse after I get my seatbelt on. "I don't know. No one's ever driven my truck but me."

"Hmm." She taps her chin but doesn't say anything else.

I drive us to a Mexican restaurant in town. "Ah, one of my favorites." She climbs out before I can reach her. She pats a hand against my chest with a smile on her lips that tells me she knew I was coming to open her door for her but chose to jump out before I could because it'd drive me insane.

But as soon as she starts walking toward the restaurant, my thoughts vanish as I watch the sway of her hips. By the time she reaches the door, I don't even notice that she's stopped and plow right into her backside.

"Shit. Sorry." I laugh, using her waist to brace myself.

"Distracted?" She smirks.

"Completely." She shakes her head as I pull the door open for her. When she steps past me, I smack her ass causing her to jump slightly.

We're seated a few minutes later, the complimentary chips and salsa are set in front of us and Lou dives right in. That's one thing I've always loved about her, she isn't afraid to eat in front of anyone. When my girl is hungry, she eats.

"How's work been going?" I ask, making small talk.

"It's been going good. Busy, which is what I like."

"Nicole looks good. Happy."

"She is," she says, delighted that I've brought her best friend up. "Roger is amazing."

"Yeah, he seemed like a good dude when we met at the reunion." I laugh, grabbing another chip from the basket. "At least what I met of him."

"You two would get along. They have three boys." I listen to her talk about each of them and it's obvious that she adores them.

"Three boys, though? Damn." I laugh, thinking back to my childhood and how mom always said I was nothing but boy and it drove her crazy. Between broken bones and pissing on the toilet seat, I'm sure she would have preferred a girl.

"It drives Nicole insane most days, but she is such a good mom."

"I can tell that. She always struck me as the mothering type."

Lou nods to agree with me, taking a bite of her chip.

We order, talk more, eat, talk some more. It's nice.

When we're back in my truck, I head out of town and turn on one of the gravels that borders the city limits sign.

"What are we doing?" she asks, a confused look crossing her face when I unbuckle and open the driver's side door.

By the time I reach her door, her eyes are wide and looking at me like I've lost my damn mind. I still don't say anything, my eyes stay on hers as I reach across her lap and unbuckle her seat belt.

"Declan." She laughs. "What are you doing? Leaving me here?"

"Like I'd ever leave you." I pull her legs to face me then lean over and kiss her lips briefly. "I'm letting you drive."

"What?" Her eyes widen, her mouth falling open with a hint of a smile. "Are you serious?"

I don't even get a chance to answer because she's jumping out, pushing me to the side and running around the front end to the driver's side.

Shaking my head, I climb into the seat she was just occupying. "Alright, go easy on he—" My head is thrown back as the truck takes off down the road, a smiling Lou is sitting close to the steering wheel because she's too short to see over the wheel.

She's fucking breathtaking and I'm the luckiest fucking man in the world.

28

LOU

It's finally the day of my parents' renewal.

When we started planning it, it seemed so far away but the days have actually flown by. Granted my time has been occupied by a certain Marine who makes me lose track of everything when we're together. I've been late for work three times, which is not the norm for me, although I can't really blame the entire thing on him since I was the one who succumbed to pleas of climbing back into bed each morning.

Things have been going well between us. He has seemed a little stressed, but I chalked it up to him being stressed about what he told me about Abigail. I can't imagine how hard that must be for him, to be a part of everything that took place. He doesn't really share much else with me that's related to the military. He's pretty tight-lipped, only telling me bits and pieces of things. Which I guess is how it's supposed to be, but I do hate not knowing everything.

I look around my parent's backyard. The lights have

been hung from the pergola, with a beautiful round table situated in the center for my parents for the reception portion. Mom wanted this to feel magical, and I think she's getting exactly what she wants with this backyard wedding.

My dad couldn't care less on how any of it looks, he just wants her. That's what he's said over and over again. I've watched the two of them over the last month, closer than I ever have before. I see Declan and myself in their relationship, the way my dad seems to track my mom's every move when they're in the same room. Declan does that with me, and it gives me butterflies every single time I catch his stare.

Walking around the backyard, I set a large vase in the center of each table and begin arranging the flowers the way I want them. It's warmer than it has been, but there's still a chill in the air. My mom is wearing a white, fur stole over her dress to provide her with some warmth.

Tessa has been a godsend with helping prepare everything, and I couldn't have done it without her. I seriously couldn't ask for a better sister-in-law than her.

Once I have the vases fixed exactly how I want them, I head toward the house to start getting ready. Decaln and his mom will be here later, and I can't wait to see him. I've been so swamped between work and getting everything ready for today that we haven't had a chance to spend as much time together as we'd like.

I am nervous about how my brother will act once he sees Declan, but I know my mom will have his ass in a heartbeat if he ruins today for her. As if my brother knew I was talking about him, he steps out of the backdoor to the house. I wave, catching his attention and he changes course to come to me.

"Hey." He scrunches his nose. "You're not wearing that are you?"

I punch him in the arm, hearing him cry from the pain I doubt I actually caused him still brings me joy after all these years. "No, you asshole. I'm changing, I was just wearing this to get everything setup."

"Thank fuck."

I roll my eyes at him.

"So, Declan's coming today?"

I suck in a deep breath, already knowing where this is going. "Yes, and please don't be a dick and ruin today for Mom or Dad."

"I'm not, it's fine. I'm actually glad he's coming."

I stare at him, waiting for a joke to come out of his mouth to follow that last statement up but nothing comes. I guess I didn't see where that was going after all.

"We talked."

"When?" I ask, Declan never said anything to me about it but then I remember, the bruising along his jaw and the cut just above my brother's eyes. "You two fought?"

"Not necessarily, it was more like a few *friendly* punches." He shrugs.

"Friendly punches? Do you think I'm dumb? Tell me what happened?"

He shakes his head, so I do what any good older sister does and I grab him by the ear, twisting until I have him in a headlock. Knowing he's going to go for my leg so he can pick me up, I wrap my leg around one of his until he starts to tap my arm.

"Alright, alright. Let me the fuck go."

"What the hell is wrong with you two?" Our dad is behind us when I release Kyle and slowly turn around.

"Lou, how many damn times do I have to tell you to leave your brother alone? Especially before family functions."

"Sorry." I kick at the grass beneath my shoe.

"And Kyle, I don't know what you did but apologize to your sister."

Kyle scoffs next to me but turns to look at me anyways. I smile, like the little vixen I am waiting for my apology.

"Sorry."

"With meaning," my dad says, making my smile grow wider as I wiggle my brows at him.

"I'm sorry."

That seems to oblige our dad, he heads back in the direction of the house. Once he's inside, I focus my attention back on Kyle.

"Spill."

He rolls his eyes, blowing out a deep breath and shoving his hands in his pocket before answering. "I ran into him at the gym, we had words, it got heated but in the end we were cool. Or as cool as we can get after everything."

"What did he tell you?" I'm curious, I didn't figure Declan would just openly share his reasoning with anyone.

"He told me why he left, that he didn't want you to live the type of life he's watched his mom live." Kyle steps closer to me, throwing an arm over my shoulder. "I think that's pretty damn admirable." He kisses my temple before letting me go and walking to where Tessa is setting the placemats on the tables.

I watch the two of them, feeling the tears begin to form in my eyes from everything Kyle's just told me. Checking the time on my watch, I realize that the ceremony will be starting soon, which means Declan is on his way and I'm still not dressed.

Rushing up the stairs, I head into my old room to change into my dress and heels. I curl my hair quickly, which is lucky for me, I have hair that is easy to fix and never takes me long. Adding a soft touch of makeup to my face, I check the mirror and make sure everything is good before heading back downstairs toward the master bedroom where my mom is.

When I walk in, my eyes fall on my mom immediately. She's stunning, and I hope like hell I'll look like her at her age. Her white dress cuts off just above the knees, the sleeves of the dress cuff around her shoulders and the necklace around her neck holds a large diamond my father gave her a few years ago for their anniversary.

"You look stunning, Mom." I smile at her, quickly closing the door behind me so my dad doesn't sneak a peek. He's been antsy all day to see her in this dress. For a man who couldn't care less about the ceremony, he's been all into the planning portion.

"Thank you." She looks back at the mirror once more before turning to me. "I can't believe after all these years, we're actually renewing our vows to one another." She giggles, holding a hand over her stomach.

"Now, Mom... don't tell me you're pregnant." I stare at her, face serious but joking with my words.

"Oh, stop it." She laughs, waving a hand at me. "He just still gives me butterflies."

"I know that feeling." The words slip past my lips before I realize what I've even said.

"I know you do." My eyes lift to hers and she's smiling. "I'm glad he's home, sweetheart."

"Me, too."

I make sure Mom has everything she needs before I head out to look for Declan and his mom, and to make sure Kyle is in place to walk our mother down the aisle. I swear, I should have hired a babysitter to keep up with him because he's worse than Lucy and Lane.

Stepping into the backyard, I see that most of the guests have begun to show up and have taken their seats in the yard. Declan and his mother are near the bar, and as if he senses my presence, his head turns, finding me instantly. I stop walking, watching as his eyes drift to my feet before slowly moving up my body, leaving every inch of me feeling as if he's just undressed me in front of all these guests.

He pushes away from the bar, causing his mom to turn in alarm before she realizes where he's heading. He stops once we're toe to toe and softly brings his lips to mine. I don't care how many people are staring, I don't care how many people are going to leave tonight and tell everyone what they saw.

People should already know that we were destined to be together.

Just me and him.

For always.

29

DECLAN

She's fucking beautiful.

The slit that dress has up the side leaves just barely enough to my imagination. But tonight, make no mistakes, she's mine.

I didn't plan to kiss her in front of everyone, not that I care what anyone thinks, but I know how the rumor mill in this town works. Plus, I didn't want to take away from her parents' big day, although I'm clearly a selfish bastard who couldn't help myself.

I never can when it comes to her.

Mom and I take our seats, waiting as the music begins for the ceremony to start. Kyle walks his wife down the aisle before walking to the outside and back to the house.

His twins walk slowly from the backdoor down the aisle, and everyone laughs when Lucy takes her time and strategically sets each petal on the ground while Lane nearly runs down the aisle not bothering to wait on his sister. The crowd laughs while Tessa walks back down the aisle and hurries Lucy along.

The doors to the house open once again, and Lou steps outside linking her arm with her brother. She's so fucking breathtaking, a damn vision in that dress. My mom has to nudge me in the side to remind me to actually breathe when I look at her. Her dark blue eyes are fixated on me, all the way down the aisle until she can no longer look at me without turning her head.

Kyle does the same as before, leaving to the side and back up to the house. Lou stands next to Tessa, with Lucy and Lane in front of her. She bends, letting Lane kiss her on the cheek before she stands and smiles at me.

That sight. Fuck, hits me right in the chest.

Mrs. Tucker steps outside, and everyone stands to watch her son walk her down the aisle. When she gets close to where my mom and I are seated, her head turns slightly as she winks at me before waving at my mother.

The rest of the ceremony is a blur, the only thing I remember from it is Lou's eyes on mine. With every word the preacher said, she portrayed it through her look and told me everything I already knew about our future.

The only problem is that I haven't told her about the possibility of me getting orders, not yet. I'm an idiot for not telling her the other night at the diner, but I was already sharing so much and I didn't want to scare her. Unsure of how she'd react to the news. I don't want to lose her, but I also still have that fear of her turning into my mother. Not that being like my mother would be bad, I just don't want her to waste her life away waiting on me. And what if something happens and I never return?

I can't do that to her.

But it's different this time and I don't know if I can fucking walk away again.

I know that if I do, it'll ruin her and me at the same time. Leaving us both broken and unable to heal from the pain that will tear through us.

Once the ceremony ends, they all walk back the direction they came, gathering under the pergola at the back of the house. Everyone stands and follows along behind them, I walk toward her parents first to give my congratulations.

"Declan Sanchez." Mr. Tucker sticks his hand out between us. "How have you been, boy?"

"I've been good, sir. You?"

He smiles, looking down at his wife as he releases my hand and wraps an arm around her shoulder, pulling her tightly against him. "I've never been better."

"Declan, thank you for coming," Mrs. Tucker says.

I lean in, giving the woman who was always like a second mother to me a hug.

"Pemela," she holds her arms out to my mother, "so glad you could make it as well. I was worried it was short notice."

"Thank you for having me." My mom smiles at her, and the two embrace in a hug. "I wouldn't have missed it."

Lou comes up behind me, pulling me away from the conversation our parents are having. "I want you to formally meet someone." She smiles, tangling her fingers with mine. "Declan, this is Tessa."

"It's nice to meet you, I've heard a lot about you." I smile, reaching a hand out to shake hers.

"Nice to meet you, too. I hope they were all good things." She smiles, looking over at Lou as Kyle walks up behind his wife and slides a hand around her waist.

"Very."

"And this..." Lou trails off, bending to her niece and nephew's level. "Is Lucy and Lane."

"It's nice to meet you both, I know your Aunt Lou sure talks about y'all a lot."

Lucy takes me by surprise and throws herself at me while Lane stares at me in confusion. They're only two, so I'm sure it's confusing for them to see Lou with someone else. Especially if Peter was in their lives. I need to ask her about that, we've not really talked a lot about Peter.

My eyes shoot to Lou's before bouncing from Tessa to Kyle to gauge how Kyle's reacting to this.

"Lucy, let's let Declan go, baby," Kyle says, touching his daughter's arm.

"No!" Lucy shouts, making everyone chuckle, including Kyle.

So I stand, with Lucy in my arms.

We spend the next couple of hours on the makeshift dance floor, dancing to every type of music you can imagine. Lucy and I share a few dances, laughing the entire time when I spin her around in circles.

Everyone started to leave about fifteen minutes ago, including my mom. I grab Lou's hand, pulling her to follow me to the dance floor. We're the only couple out here, besides her parents. They've barely stopped dancing all evening, enjoying their time together.

I pull Lou to my chest, wrapping my arms around her lower back as I begin to sway to the beat of the song. Elvis Presley's *Can't Help Falling In Love* surrounds us. It's a song I've heard a million times in her house, it's one of her mom's favorites, but this time it's like I'm hearing it for the first time all over again.

Lou rests her forehead against my chest, while I sing

the lyrics to her and feel the chill bumps break out across her skin. It's dark now, so the only light I have is from the twinkling lights hung around the yard.

The song changes, but we don't break apart, we continue dancing to a few more until she spins in my arms and her ass is pressed against my dick that's now hardening. She notices, because she continues wiggling her ass against me until a groan barrels past my lips and I spin her in my arms.

"Did I tell you how much I love that red lipstick on you?"

She slowly shakes her head.

"Or how I haven't stopped thinking about how those lips would look wrapped around my cock?"

A small gasp comes from her, bringing a smirk to my lips as I watch her look around us to make sure no one's listening. I lean into her, brushing my lips across her ear to make sure only she can hear this last part.

"All I want to do right now, baby, is drag you off this dance floor and into your old bedroom and make that a reality."

"Declan," she whispers, letting her hand run down my chest until it stops just above my hardened dick. "I'm ready to go."

I wink, pulling her in front of me as we leave the dance floor. The last thing I need right now is for her parents to see me with a fucking hard on on their renewal night. We say our goodbye's, quickly, before we're climbing in her car and I'm driving to her place.

Traffic laws don't matter to me right now. The only thing on my mind is how her pussy is going to taste when we step inside in a few minutes.

As soon as I pull into her garage bay, she's out of the car and rushing through the door. I chase behind her, barely remembering to hit the garage control by the door before I burst through the door after her. By the time I make it to her room, she's already trying to unzip her dress but I shake my head.

That slit up the side has driven me fucking crazy all night, and I'm about to enjoy this fantasy coming true. She looks confused as I step closer to her, reaching around to her back before dropping to my haunches. My eyes stay locked on hers while I run my hands up her bare thigh, pulling the dress to the side to hook my fingers in her lace thong and slowly slide it down her legs.

She watches, biting at her bottom lip the entire time. That sight only fuels my need to taste her more. She lifts each leg, stepping out of the lace fabric. I run my hand back up the inside of her leg until I reach her center.

"Fuck, you're so wet."

Her eyes flash with hunger as I slide a finger in her pussy, followed by another, and another. She widens her legs, giving me the entrance I need to send her over the edge. I watch as her head falls back while my fingers continue to bring those sexy little moans from her lips. Sliding her dress to the side, I lean forward letting my tongue slide over her clit and smile against her as she shivers, latching onto my hair.

I grind my nose down into her clit and chuckle as her moans grow louder before forcing myself away from her.

Her cries of disappointment make me smile as I stand to my full height and begin to unbuckle my belt. Once I've rid my body of clothes, I turn her away from me and slowly unzip her dress until she's completely nude in front of me. The curve of her ass has me so fucking hard, it's painful.

I pull her hair to one side of neck before taking her hips and guiding her forward onto the mattress until she's on her hands and knees in front of me. Her pink pussy on display, only for me.

I step forward, climbing onto my knees until my cock brushes against her sex. She looks over her shoulder, those blue eyes sparkle for what's to come.

"I've wanted to do this all fucking night," I tell her, rubbing my cock over her slick entrance.

"Please," she begs, moving her hips side to side to entice me. And it fucking works.

I lean forward, the head of my cock finding her entrance like a fucking magnet as I slowly ease inside of her until I'm buried all the way to the hilt.

She feels fucking perfect.

But that's what she is after all. Perfection.

I slowly pull out, watching as her sex stretches around my dick before I slam back in. She rocks backwards, urging me on with each thrust.

She's tight, so tight that I can feel my orgasm building already.

I continue to pump my hips into her, giving her everything she asks for without using any of the words to ask. My hand slides over her damp skin, all the way down to her ass before I slap it once, leaving a pink handprint in its place.

"Fuck," I cry out, that sight alone has my head falling to my shoulders in pleasure. "You're so fucking tight, baby."

When I open my eyes again, she's shifted her weight with an arm reaching under her. I use my hand to follow along her arm and find her fingers moving over her clit, and that's all it takes for me to lose control.

My orgasm slams into me just as her pussy starts to convulse around me. I collapse onto her, using my forearms to keep my weight from crushing her. Our bodies are slick with sweat, and my heart is thudding through my chest.

"It gets better each time," she whispers into the comforter of her bed. "How does it get better?"

"It's all you, babe. All you." I kiss the back of her neck before pulling myself up. The cool air hits my skin when I pull free from her.

"I love you," she says, rolling over with her pussy back on display for me.

And just like that, I'm hard again.

30

LOU

THE FIRST THING I notice when I wake up is the feeling of Declan's arm around my waist and the steady beat of his heart against my back. I'm so warm, wrapped in his arms, that I don't even want to pay attention to my screaming bladder right now.

Pulling the cover back slowly, I start to stand when I feel his arm tighten around me. "Don't get up." His deep, husky voice is full of sleep but he's able to pull me back against him.

"I have to pee." I laugh, trying to remove his arm.

"You know what I heard?"

"What?" I ask, halting my movement.

"That orgasms are more intense when your bladder is full." He presses a kiss just under my ear, and his arm starts to move lower until it's resting against my thigh.

My breathing picks up, like it always does with his touch.

"I like you in my shirt, without any panties on..." he

trails off, letting his hand slide to my ass before moving lower to my sex.

The feeling of his fingers near my center makes me wet, wanting more of his touch. Lifting my leg, I give him the access that both of us want and a moan escapes my lips when his fingers brush through my lips.

"So, fucking wet." He shifts his weight so that he's leaning on his elbow and looking into my eyes. "Always so fucking wet for me."

His words fuel my need for him, and when his finger slips inside me, I pull away. This time, it frustrates him and I can't help but smile at the look on his face. He thinks I'm about to get up, but instead, I slide under the comforter and settle between his legs. My fingers wrap around his long length, moving up and down before taking the tip of his cock in my mouth. I let my tongue swirl circles until his hand grabs the back of my head, driving his dick deeper into my throat.

I work him up, squeezing his balls with each stroke of my mouth until he's about to lose control and yanks my mouth free. He pulls me up his chest, giving me a smile that fucking stops my heart before crushing his lips to mine.

"Did you like that?" I ask, in between kisses.

"I fucking loved it." He pulls my legs apart so that I'm straddling him and lines his cock up with my pussy before driving in so hard that the room nearly spins.

I could never get used to this feeling, it's more than we've ever shared before. Each time with Declan gets more intense, and I fucking love it. It was never like this with Peter, something was always lacking and there was never emotion. But with Declan, we share all of our emotions, the pain, the love, the regret, every time we touch. Each kiss seals something different for us.

His fingers dig into my thighs as I rise and fall on him, the sound of his moans only makes me work faster. When I grind my clit against him, I send myself spiraling out of control. The orgasm ripping through my body is unlike anything I've ever experienced before. The room nearly goes black from the intense pleasure coursing through my body.

"Declan!" I cry out, as he pounds into my wet pussy until he finds his own release.

I feel his cock stretch before exploding into me, drawing out my orgasm in a pleasure of pain until I collapse onto him. Neither of us move as we try to catch our breath, the sound of his rapid heart beat is the only thing I hear while his hand rubs circles along my lower back.

He's right, sex with a full bladder is more intense.

Finally, I climb off of him and walk to the bathroom to clean up. When I'm finished, I climb back into bed while he does the same.

"I'm going to take a quick shower," he says, before shutting the bathroom door. A second later the shower comes on so I grab the remote from the night stand and turn on the last episode of *Grey's Anatomy* that I missed.

Declan's phone chimes, but I don't pay attention to it, keeping my focus on the drama unfolding on the screen. When his phone chimes three more times, I pick it up to make sure there isn't an emergency.

There's a name I don't recognize on the screen, but it's the text message that causes my heart to feel like it's breaking all over again.

Commander: *You leave in twenty-four hours.*

Twenty-four hours? Where the hell is he going?

I shove open the bathroom door, not caring that he's naked when I confront him, not caring that he's in the middle of a shower and I should wait to calm down before having this discussion. But right now, I'm being fueled by the scared eighteen year old girl who felt like her world ended fifteen years ago.

"Coming to jo–" He looks at me, realizing how pissed off I am. "What's wrong?"

I don't speak as he slides open the glass shower door, stepping out to grab his towel all while never looking away from me.

"When were you going to tell me you were leaving?" I ask, handing him his phone. It's the one question that could ruin this entire thing we have going again. "When?" I ask again, watching as he reads the text message he just received.

"I was going to tell you, baby. I promise." He steps forward but I take a step back, knowing that if he touches me I'll melt and nothing will get resolved. It's taking everything in my power not to cry in front of him right now.

"When, Declan?" My voice is raised and I watch as his head tilts back slightly from my outburst.

"I don't know." He drops his head, tossing his phone on to the bathroom vanity.

"You don't know? That's all you're going to say?"

"This is why we can't work," he says.

Those six little words send my world crashing around me. I can feel the moment my heart actually chips in my chest and the pain is nearly unbearable.

"Declan."

"I can't be fucking there, with you here. It won't work."
He steps around me and back into the bedroom. I follow
behind him, trying to form a thought that will make sense.
I don't want us to end, I just want him to think about what
he's saying. I'm upset at the fact that he didn't tell me he
was being deployed, and hid it from me for God knows
how long. I'm upset that I had to find out about it from a
text message and not from him. And I'm upset that he's
doing the same fucking shit he did fifteen years ago, rather
than talking this out with me.

"Declan, stop. We can talk about this, I'm only upset
bec–"

"Because you know this won't work." He pulls his shirt
over his head before grabbing his jeans. "If you're here,
alone without me for months on end, you'll slowly lose a
piece of yourself waiting and wondering if I'll even come
home. I didn't fucking want this to happen, I didn't want
to deploy again, but I don't have a choice this time. I do
but I don't," he says and I frown at his words. "I can't say
no to this mission, I need to go. It's what I was born
to do."

With that, he walks out of the bedroom door, leaving
me with tears streaming down my face and a heart that will
never be healed again.

I hear the front door slam, and know that he isn't
coming back to talk about this, so I do the only thing I can
right now. I grab my phone and call the one person that I
know will never walk away from me.

I send my brother a text that tells him I need him. I'm
unable to answer when he calls, but I know he'll come right
away so I just toss my phone back to the bed and collapse
to the floor. I replay what just happened over and over in

my mind. If I had approached him differently would it have changed the outcome?

Why does he feel like we can't work?

A few minutes later, Kyle finds me in the same spot I was in when Declan stormed out. I'm on my knees, with tears that just won't stop no matter how hard I try.

Kyle pushes the door open, halting for only a minute until his eyes focus on me. "What the fuck happened?"

"He—" I hiccup. "He, he left me again." I cry harder this time.

"What? I need you to calm down, sweetheart. Talk to me." He holds me, allowing me time to get my emotions under control before I speak again.

"He is being deployed and didn't tell me." I sob into his chest, the pain feeling just like I remember it.

"Shit." he mutters, wrapping both arms around me. "Where is he?"

"I don't know, he left right before I called you. He didn't tell me he was getting deployed, Kyle." My brother brushes some of the hair from my face, which is difficult considering it's sticking to the wetness of my tears. "I was upset that he didn't tell me and then he told me we'd never work."

"It'll be okay," Kyle whispers, rocking us both back and forth. "Shh."

The only problem is... I'm not sure if I'll ever be okay.

I don't know if Declan will ever come back. I don't know what my future holds right now.

31

DECLAN

FUCK!

I fucked up. Big time. Worse than I did fifteen fucking years ago.

Why couldn't I just tell her that this is it for me? I'm doing this one deployment and coming home to her for good. I'm ending my military career so that I can be with her.

Or, I was. I'm not sure there is an us at this point. I walked out without even looking back, knowing that I'd see her tears and go running to take them away. I couldn't do it. I know that I'm needed for this mission, and that it will be a long one to clean up, probably a year if not longer.

I have a duty to this country, and that means the people in it. If the rumors are true, and there are hostages being held against their will, then it's my team that will be able to save them.

I won't be able to live with myself if I don't follow through on this. My dumb ass should have tried to explain that to Lou, given her something to look forward to or some type of explanation for doing what I'm doing.

But what do I do instead? I fucking ruin it just like I always do.

I overreacted and spoke without thinking. Saying the words that I knew would get her attention and make her not chase after me.

When I get to my house, I sit on the front porch for a while, getting lost in my thoughts of how fucked up this situation has become. My mom and aunt pull in a few minutes later, but I don't wait to chat with them, instead I grab Gunnar's leash and head down the street with him, attempting to clear my head. I leave tomorrow morning, and I need to be at the top of my game if I'm even going to attempt to return home in the future.

Gunnar and I walk for hours, passing people we know but I can't even bring myself to look at them. I feel numb inside, a feeling I know all too well. After my legs feel like they're going to give out and Gunnar is struggling to keep up, we make the turn heading back to my mom's house.

I'm relieved when I see my aunt's car gone, at least I won't have to deal with her. Pushing through the door, I unhook Gunnar's leash and watch as he runs to his corner of the living room and collapses against his dog bed. My mom leans up in her chair, eying me cautiously before asking, "What happened?"

"I fucked up." I cringe at my word choice but she doesn't say anything. "I ended it with Lou."

She sucks in a deep breath, but keeps her eyes trained on my face. I have to look away, I can't say this next part and see the reaction it brings.

"I'm leaving in less than twenty-four hours. I don't know where to yet, just that I'll be gone for a year, maybe longer."

"You stupid, foolish man." My eyes snap back to hers. "I've watched you over the last fifteen years, create a career that your father would be proud of, but ruin a life that you could have had at the same time." She pauses. "Lou is your soulmate, and you keep pushing her away. You won't get another chance like this, Declan. She forgave you for what you did in the past, but breaking her this time will be too much to overcome."

"Mom," I take a step closer to her but she halts me by holding a hand up.

"No." She stands, shaking her head. "This won't bring back your father, Declan."

"I know!" I shout. "I fucking know this won't bring him back. He's dead, Mom. I know that."

"Then why the hell do you keep doing this to yourself? Keep causing yourself so much heartache for this idea in your head of being closer to him?" she asks.

"I haven't felt close to him in a long time, Mom. I don't know..." I trail off, trying to gather my thoughts.

"You're going to lose her for good this time."

"I know that." I shake my head, the sound of laughter floating from my lips. "Maybe it's for the better."

"And that, my boy, is why you are stupid and foolish." She doesn't say anything else as she walks out of the room and down the hall to her own room.

"Goddamn it!" I shout, making Gunnar jump from my outburst. I cringe, waiting for my mom to come back down the hallway to give me another ass chewing, and when she doesn't, I realize just how much I have fucked up.

I storm down the hallway, slamming my door shut behind me before collapsing onto my bed. The slow spinning of the ceiling fan eventually helps me drift off to sleep.

———

THE NEXT MORNING, my eyes snap open but slam shut just as quickly from the pain the light filtering through the curtain brings.

Everything from yesterday slams into me at once, bringing on a headache from hell. But maybe that's what I deserve. Raising myself from the bed, I run a hand over my face before looking over the room, my eyes settling on the one picture that I've never been able to take down.

Standing, I pull my shirt from my head and toss it to the floor before heading to the bathroom for a quick shower. I need to be at the airport soon, my flight will leave in a few hours and I still have to pack.

I stand in the shower, letting the hot water glide over my sore muscles and think of all the things I'll be missing soon. The things I'm giving up to go do this assignment. The things I may never get back, no, that I know I'll never get back.

Coming home and rekindling things with Lou is something I never in my wildest dreams thought would happen again. I was sure that I had hurt her so much that she would set fire to me as soon as she saw me, but I'm glad it went the other direction. But now, I feel like I've hurt her all over again and that's like acid on my fucking tongue.

Turning the knob, I shut the water off and head back into my room. I'm dressed in my Combat Uniform when my mom pokes her head in. Her eyes are red lined, and I know she's spent most of the evening crying over our argument.

Dropping the clothes in my hand, I cross the room as she pushes the door the rest of the way open, and wrap her in my arms. "I'm sorry, Momma," I say, resting my cheek against the top of her head.

"I know, baby. I am, too. I didn't want you to leave upset with me." She cries into my chest.

It's odd how things change, I still remember being the little boy that would hold her the way she's holding me.

"I'm not upset with you, I could never be upset with you," I tell her, squeezing her a little tighter. "I love you, Mom."

"I love you, too." She pulls away from me, looking up at me in the process. Her eyes move from mine to the bed where my bag is half packed. "Are you going to go talk to her before you leave?"

I step away from her, returning to what I was doing and shake my head in the process. "I can't," I mutter. The thought of how she must be feeling right now is burning in my chest, the image of her tear filled eyes when I told her we couldn't do this is etched into my brain and I know it'll never go away.

I'm such an asshole.

Lou... my beautiful, perfect, Lou.

"Okay." She smiles weakly at me. "I'll be in the living room with Gunnar."

I nod and watch as she slowly backs out of the doorway and pulls the door shut behind her, leaving me in the silence of my thoughts.

I think of my dad, wondering what he would do in this

situation? How did he leave Mom time and time again, knowing that it was breaking her on the inside? How did he do it all with such pride? I love my career, and I'm damn lucky I get to be one of the ones protecting this country, but I'd be lying if I didn't say it fucking sucked sometimes.

Each and every time I think of Lou, I have to remind myself that this is what's for the best. Her being here, moving on with her life, and even though that's a hard pill to swallow, I hope she finds someone that loves her and takes care of her in all the ways I'd never be able to.

I get everything else I need packed in my back and do one last scan around the room. My eyes land on that same picture, the one with the wind blowing Lou's hair all those years ago. I pull it from the wall, running a thumb over her face before tucking it into my back pocket. Grabbing Gunnar's leash, I throw my bag over my shoulder and head into the living room.

My mom is in her chair, with Gunnar's head laying across her lap. "Gunnar, come." He stands, moving away from my mom and to me. I drop to my knees, grabbing both sides of his shoulders and rubbing. "You be a good boy," I tell him, and I swear it's like he understands what I'm saying because he nods his head just a little.

My mom stands from her seat and comes over to me. I hand her the leash in my hand. "He'll take care of you while I'm gone, okay?"

"You come back to me, okay?" she says.

"I will come back, Mom. I promise." I give her my word.

"Don't make promises you can't keep," she warns me.

It's the same thing she used to tell my dad when he

would leave, his response was always the same. He'd chuckle, walk over to her and kiss her nose.

"I'll do my best," I promise.

"I know you will." She wraps her arms around me, squeezing me tightly one last time before I walk out the front door.

The cab is parked in front of the house as I make my way down the driveway. The driveway that is now full of the overgrowing grass and looks like a gravel drive should, all thanks to Lou.

The memory of that day causes my chest to ache. I open the backdoor of the cab, throwing my back inside first. Turning toward the house, I see my mom standing on the porch, waving while wiping away her tears and Gunnar at her side watching through the screen door.

I hate that I'm causing her this much pain, but I have a duty to uphold, and one I plan to follow through with so I can hang my hat up for good.

This is it for me. Even if Lou isn't in the picture, I can't keep doing this to my mom. Last night was an eye opener for me, but I also feel like I need this last deployment to make peace with my decision. So that I can lay rest to whatever closeness I thought I would find when I joined.

———

I SIT, waiting for my flight to board while scrolling through my Facebook app on my phone. I'm missing Gunnar right now, but my mom needs him.

My eyes continue to scan the screen, making sure I don't miss boarding while I wait. A Starbucks is across from where I'm sitting, and I watch as each person slowly makes their way through the line before I decide to get up and grab a cup. Maybe it'll help with my piss poor attitude and give me something else to focus on than the bleeding heart in my chest.

I expected to have a message, a call, fucking anything from Lou but she's been silent since I walked away from her. And really, I don't blame her. If I was in her shoes, I'd do the same fucking thing and forget about my ass.

She deserves better than that, better than me. She always has.

"Are you in line?" a soft voice asks from beside me.

Turning my head, I see a small blonde with her hair in a messy bun on top of her head. She has blue eyes and a face full of makeup that does absolutely nothing for me. She's pretty, sure, but there's only one shade of blue I'm interested in, and I don't think anyone else on the planet has it. *Only her.*

"Yeah, sorry." I take a step toward the person in front of me, I had gotten lost in my own thoughts again and didn't notice the line moving. I force Lou from my mind, ordering my coffee when it's my turn and walking back to where I was waiting before.

Taking my first sip, I let the hot liquid burn and relish in the pain as it slides down my throat. At least I'm feeling something, right?

"Where are you heading?" That voice. The same one from moments ago. I don't respond immediately and she moves to stand in front of me. "I'm heading out to Vegas." She smiles and points toward a group of women, all dressed similar to her. You know the type, the ones who pretend to dress comfortably but you can tell it's more about the look than actually being comfortable. "My friend's getting married in a few weeks so we're having a Bachelorette party."

"Congratulations to your friend." I expect her to walk away when I don't indulge anymore information on where I'm heading, but she doesn't budge from her spot.

"So, what's your name?" She bites her bottom lip and that alone annoys me. There's only one girl that can affect me with that move, and she isn't the one in front of me.

"Declan." I nod, lifting my cup for another drink. I don't offer to shake her hand or greet her in anyway, because she's grating on my nerves and I just want to be left the fuck alone right now.

"I'm Lily."

I tip my head when one of her friends calls her name. She turns her head but doesn't make any effort to move so I do. I step around her, not giving her another look and head toward the wall of windows to watch as they work on loading the plane.

"Declan!" a voice cuts through the air. *Her* voice. I'd recognize it anywhere. When I turn my head, I nearly drop my coffee at the sight of her. She's fucking breathtaking, even when she looks like she's barely slept and her eyes are red and puffy from tears I've caused.

Our last conversation runs through my mind.

This is why we can't work.

Fuck, I was horrible to her. I wish I could explain everything that's going on in my head, in a way that makes sense and doesn't make me sound like a fucking lunatic. She gave me a second chance, a chance that I sure as hell didn't deserve but because she's so perfect and so pure, she gave her heart to me again, all so I could shatter it.

I can't be fucking there, with you here. It won't work.

Because you know this won't work.

It's what I was born to do.

What I was born to do. The biggest lie I've ever told.

What I was born to do, is be the man this woman deserves.

I HAVEN'T GOTTEN out of bed since Kyle tucked me into it yesterday. I'm sure I smell, my hair's a mess from catching all my tears while I've laid here and cried. I've switched my pillows out, one after another, after getting each soaking wet from the overflow of my emotions pouring out of me.

The picture of Declan's face when he told me he couldn't do this, that it wasn't going to work with him being there and me being here, is constantly playing on repeat in my mind. Slowly torturing me.

I tried to fall asleep last night, but each time I woke up a few minutes later crying so hard I couldn't breath. The pain that radiates through my entire body is unlike anything I've ever felt before.

This time was different, I gave him everything, even when I told myself I shouldn't because this was always a possibility. He had all the power to break me, and in the end that's exactly what he did.

I guess Kyle told Nicole about last night; she's called

and texted constantly to check on me, but I can't find it in me to return anything yet. I'm so weak.

I hear my garage door open, and I'm hoping it's someone in my family or Nicole... but maybe if it's someone here to rob me they can put me out of my misery. That thought vanishes as quickly as it came when Tessa pokes her head in my cracked door before seeing that I'm awake and pushes it open.

"Hi," she says, stepping inside and kicking her shoes off. She's dressed in a cream colored sweatpants and a long sleeve t-shirt that matches. "How are you feeling?"

Her words bring a mount of emotions back to the surface and the tears begin to fall while I hiccup trying to catch my breath again. It's like this each time. I'm able to slowly calm down enough, and then one thought brings it all crashing back in.

"Oh, Lou." She rounds the bed, climbing in beside me and wraps herself around me, holding me tightly against her while I fall apart. "It's okay. Shh." Her hand runs through my hair while the other holds my head against her chest.

My brother got so lucky with Tessa, and I'm blessed to be able to call her my sister now.

"I just don't understand." I cry, not sure if I'm talking to Tessa or to myself.

"Don't understand what?"

"How he can walk away. Again." I wipe at my eyes. "He says he doesn't want me to be here, worried about him. I guess he thinks I can't handle being away from him, or being with someone in the military."

"Can you?" she asks.

I think about her question, wondering if I could. It's a

sacrifice, but I'd do anything for Declan. I'm not sure why he doesn't see that.

"Yes," I say, my eyes meeting hers. "I know I can. It would suck, but I could do it because at the end of the day, it would mean the two of us were together, even though we'd be miles apart." I clutch my chest. "We'd still be together."

"Have you told him that you could do this?"

"Yes," I say, but then think about it. I'm not sure if I ever did tell him I could do this. "No, I guess I didn't."

"If being with Declan is something you want, truly want, and he makes you happy... despite all the shit that's happened between the two of you, then you owe it to yourself to at least tell him that." She pauses, brushing the matted hair from my cheeks. "If he's not willing to do that then, then you can find peace in knowing you tried. It wasn't always smooth sailing between your brother and I."

I perk up at the mention of their relationship. I know it wasn't easy, finding out you're pregnant with no family couldn't be easy, but then being pregnant by one of the most well known bachelor's around here is a tough pill to swallow, but I thought the two of them had an instant connection and just fell in love... you know like in the romance books?

"There were times when I wasn't sure our kids would have their parents together. It was so new, and Kyle and I didn't know each other from our own asses." She giggles and I can't help but join in. "There's that smile." She sighs. "But, he finally told me what he wanted, and I'm so glad he did. I think I was too scared of what would happen if I expressed how I felt... because let's be honest, it's crazy to fall for someone that you had a one night stand with and just happened to get pregnant by."

"I had no idea," I admit.

"There is no simple love story," she tells me. "Love will always get complicated, because if it's simple, there is no love."

"You're a real poet." I laugh, but her words resonate with me. Our love story has never been simple and always complicated.

"I know, it's a shame I'm a realtor... I could have really gone places, you know?" I laugh at her antics. "What do you say?"

"I think I'm going to go talk to him." I turn my head away from her, the nerves coursing through my body nearly make me cry again. I'm anxious and have no fucking clue what I'm going to say to him, but she's right... I have to tell him I can do this and if he still doesn't want to then that'll be it for me. I'll have my peace.

"No offense, but maybe you should like... brush your teeth, change your clothes, and..." she trails off, waving her hands around my head. "Do something about *that*."

I laugh.

"Yeah, but maybe if I just show up like this he'll be so stunned he won't know how to argue." I throw the covers off me, trying to stand but get dizzy from being in bed for so long.

"How about I drive you?" Tessa asks, holding onto my arm.

"Yeah, okay."

———

TESSA DOESN'T TALK on the way to Declan's mom's house. She's quiet, and I'm thankful for it. I go over what I'm going to say to him in my head at least a thousand times but can't quite get it exactly how I want it.

I don't know why expressing your emotions is so damn difficult sometimes. I know what I want to say, what I want him to see, I just can't seem to get the words right in my head.

I point to Declan's house, and wait as Tessa slowly pulls in. Once she shifts her car into park, she turns to face me. "You've got this. Just tell him how you feel, make him see how strong you are."

I nod, trying to pump myself up but psych myself out instead. "I can't do this. Oh my God, I can't do this. What if he's right, what if I'm not strong enough?"

"Snap out of it." She snaps her fingers in my face. "You are so strong, he doesn't get to determine that for you."

"You're right, you're right," I say, grabbing onto the door handle and pushing the door open. "Are you right?" I pause, turning to look at her for confirmation.

"Of course I'm right." She smiles and pushes at my shoulder to get me out of the car. "Now, go!" she shouts. "I'll be right here waiting."

"Okay, okay." I shut the door and walk through the grass to their front door, hoping that he'll even open the door for me. I laugh to myself, remembering the day I came for dinner and how Gunnar took me to the ground, covering me in his muddy paw prints. And the day I helped him with the repairs to his mom's house. I look down at the gravel drive as my feet crunch the rocks beneath me with each step I take to the door. It wasn't that long ago, but at the same time it feels like a lifetime ago now.

My foot lifts and just as I step onto the first step, the front door opens and Declan's mom stands on the other side with Gunnar at her knees. "Hi, Lou." Her voice is low and soft. She's been crying and I immediately worry that I've come at a bad time.

"Can I see Declan, please?" I ask, bringing my hands together in front of me and twiddle them anxiously.

"Honey, he's gone." She chokes on her words. "He left about thirty minutes ago."

"Gone? Already?"

"His flight leaves in about an hour and a half," she tells me.

I don't respond, I turn and run back toward the car. Tessa sees me and sits up a little straighter in her seat when I yank on the door and climb in beside her.

"Take me to the airport."

Tessa nods and shifts the car into reverse and floors it out of Mrs. Sanchez's driveway, heading toward the airport. If Kyle saw how she was driving right now, he'd lose his fucking mind and kick both of our asses but I don't care. I have to make it there before he leaves, I have to.

Tessa doesn't ask any questions, she just drives. Weaving in and out of traffic like a mad woman until we reach the exit for the airport. The traffic is a madhouse, like always, and the longer we wait the more anxious I get.

"Just let me out here," I say, grabbing the handle.

"Lou, we're almost—" I throw the door open and climb out, not listening to anything she's saying and run toward the entrance of the airport.

Someone takes pity on me the closer I get and holds open the door while I rush through, scanning the area trying to figure out where he could be. I'm not even sure where he's going, I didn't bother to ask his mom any questions and I doubt he'd answer my calls or texts right now. I should have asked, I could get to him quicker.

I head in the direction that I know he'd have to be while waiting for flights to board but I'm stopped with a hand to my shoulder. "Ma'am, you can't go past this point without a ticket."

"I just need to tell someone something, please."

The woman looks at me, pity in her eyes but I can tell she's a stickler for her job and isn't going to let me pass. "I'm sorry, purchase a ticket or you won't be able to go any further."

I nod, and take a few steps backwards toward the ticket counter. I have to wait while a few others get their tickets, and when it's my turn the woman behind the counter is probably ready to hit the panic button.

I'm wearing sweats, my hair is in the biggest messy bun I think I've ever worn thanks to all the matted tangles from last night and this morning. I have little to no makeup on, except for the stained mascara that I didn't take the time to wash off all the way because I was in a hurry to get to Declan.

"Lou?" I turn at the sound of my name and see Tim.

"Tim, hi."

He stares at me, his eyes taking in a sight that he's never seen.

A very distraught Lou that appears to be falling apart.

"Are you okay?" he asks.

"I'm fine," I say, turning back to the woman staring at me. "I need your cheapest flight to anywhere."

She nods, and slowly begins tapping at the screen. I

slide my credit card over to her, not listening as she rattles off a price and looks at Tim.

"I'm trying to find Declan."

"Oh," he smiles, "I knew you two would end up back together eventually."

"Yeah?" I tilt my head, surprised to hear him say that.

"Yeah, what you two shared in high school is unlike anything I've ever seen." He raises his hand above him and scratches the back of his head. "I wish I had that."

The woman slides the ticket and my card across the counter to me. "If I don't go right now, I won't have that."

Tim doesn't say anything, he just steps aside and holds an arm out for me to pass. I smile and walk hastily toward the woman that stopped me before. With a smile, she takes my ticket and scans it before handing it back.

"Go find him."

My brows crease, but slowly smooth back out when I start to smile and push past the barrier holding me back. I throw my purse into a bin and wait to be waved through while they check everything in my bag.

Granted, all they're going to find is a few old Tic Tacs and a million bobby pins that I can't find when I actually need them.

I slide my shoes back on once I've walked through and grab my bag, shoving everything back inside and rush toward the waiting areas. I scan the crowds, looking for the man that makes my heart beat a little faster and the only one with the power to heal my broken and shattered heart.

Moving from lounge to lounge, I scan them quickly but come up short when I don't see him in any of them. My shoulders fall with defeat, and I can feel my knees getting ready to give out when he steps out of the small Starbucks with a coffee in his hand.

He is wearing his combat uniform, and looks sexy as sin in it. I watch as he takes a drink, his eyes closing tightly while he does. A small blonde walks out of the coffee shop, stopping next to him and begins talking to him.

Normally, this is the part where I'd lose it... I'd march over there and demand she get away from my man. That's what he is afterall, *my man.*

But I can tell by the way he's hardly looking at her that he isn't interested. I watch their exchange a little longer until he steps away and heads for the large windows.

"Declan!" I shout, catching his attention.

He turns, and when his eyes focus in on who's called his name, shock registers on his face. His bag drops to the floor, and he begins walking toward me, his eyes never breaking from mine.

"What are you doing here?" he asks, closing the distance between us until we're nearly chest to chest.

"I'm here for you," I whisper, looking up into his eyes, trying to read anything I can from them.

"For me?"

"Yes, I can do this, Declan. Me here, you there. I can do it."

He starts to shake his head but I grab his coffee and sit it on a nearby seat before taking both hands in mine.

"I can do this, Declan. You don't get to decide what I can handle." I fight the tears that are threatening to fall. "What I can't do, is be without you for another minute, allowing myself to get consumed in the misery of not having you in my life. I love you, D. I always have, and I always will." I squeeze. "You may be thousands of miles away from me, and it will be hard, but I'll be happy knowing that I have you at the end of the day. That you're mine and we'll have this life together when you get home."

"Lou, I can't ask you to sacrifice any more for me."

I shake my head, about to speak but he cuts me off.

"I can't let you wonder if or when I'm coming home, it'll consume you."

"*You* consume me, Declan. *You.* Nothing else. I've thought about this, about everything that it would mean to wait on you. And I want it all, Declan. Let us have it all, together," I plead. "Please don't ruin us again, you said it once that it's the biggest regret you have, don't make the same mistake twice, please."

He looks away from me, eyes floating around the airport. People have started to watch our exchange. I can see him battling within himself right now, so I do the one thing that I know can show him how much I'm willing to make this work. The heartache, the pain, the fear.

Lifting up, I turn his chin to me and press my lips against his for one of the most epic kisses of my lifetime. It's only fitting it's with Declan Sanchez. His arms wrap around me instinctively, and the crowd around us melts away as our lips seek eachother out.

With each pass of his lips, I feel him slowly giving in. I feel his love, his regret, his relief, his hopefulness, all in this kiss and I hope like hell he can feel mine too.

This is the man I'm going to marry, the one I want to have children with and experience all of life's ups and downs with. I break the kiss, resting my forehead against his.

"All I want is you... nothing more. I want every single piece of you, the good, the bad, the ugly, all of it. I don't care that you are getting ready to leave, I don't care that it may be months before I see you again. I just want you," I tell him, begging him to see the truth in my words.

"Fuck," he whispers against my lips, kissing me once more before pulling me into a hug. He squeezes me so tight, it's nearly impossible to breathe, but I don't say anything because I know he needs this right now. "I love you so fucking much, Lou. And I don't deserve you, not a single bit of you." He pulls back, looking into my eyes and frames my face with his hands. "I'm so sorry, baby. I just didn't want to cause you the pain and heartache of waiting on me. I overreacted and let my fear of losing you drive a wedge between us anyways."

"It's okay, babe. I'm here." I grab his wrists. "I'm here and I'm not going anywhere."

"I promise there will never be a day again that I do this to you. You have no idea how much you mean to me, baby." He pulls me back into his chest, kissing the top of my head. "Never again."

He holds me tightly until the crowd around us starts cheering and yelling for us both. I duck my head, feeling the embarrassment creep up my cheeks. The deep chuckle from Declan is all I hear as I tune out the crowd around us and try not to die from my discomfort of making out with my boyfriend in the middle of the airport.

An announcement breaks through the crowd, and everyone quiets down to listen. His flight is boarding, and I knew this moment would come and he'd have to leave me but it still sucks all the same.

He pulls my attention to him, stroking my cheek softly and brings my lips to his where he captivates my lips with one more toe curling kiss before he breaks away and grabs his bag.

"I'll call you," he says, walking backwards to where they're beginning to board the plan. "I love you, Lou. I'll come home to you."

"I know you will." I smile. "I love you more."

He shakes his head with a smile before turning and walking down the long tunnel to the plane.

———

ONE **W**EEK *Later*
Declan:
Hey baby. I miss you so fucking much. It's hot as shit here. I can't talk long, but I just wanted to send you a quick email and tell you I love you and I can't wait to be back home to you. I'm dreading the holidays without you.
Love always,
D.

ONE **M**ONTH **L**ATER: *December*
Lou:
Hi! Gosh, I can't believe it's already been a month. I've kept myself busy with work, and I have scheduled girls' nights so that's been fun. Have you heard anything yet about when you'll be coming home? I miss you! I love you.
Merry Christmas!
Yours always,
Lou.

. . .

SIX MONTHS LATER: *June*
Declan:
Hi Baby, it's been rough over here. I can't go into too much detail, but I've never been more scared to not return home. You're all I think about every day. I brought that picture of you with me, the one that's been on my wall for years. I keep it in my pocket all day and under my pillow at night. It's what's keeping me going.
I love you.
Your one and only,
D.

FIVE MONTHS LATER: *November*
Declan:
Hey Baby, I just got word that I'll be coming home, but I won't be there for Christmas. Which fucking sucks because I wanted to spend the holiday with you. But, I'll be home soon enough, babe. I can't wait to hold you in my arms, I fucking miss you.
Love you forever,
D.

ONE MONTH LATER: *December*
Lou:
Hi Babe, any word on your exact return date? I want to make sure I take off from work for a few days so I can soak you up. God, I've missed you. I will say

though, this year has flown by but drug at the same time. I'm so excited that you're coming home. I love you so much!

I've got to get back to work, let me know when you know something.
All yours,
Lou.

THREE DAYS LATER: *December*
Lou:
Hi baby, checking in. I didn't hear back from you. I'm kind of worried, but I'm hoping you're just busy. It's Christmas Eve and I wish so badly you were here to help me wrap all these presents for the kids. Although, I probably went a little overboard. Surprise, surprise. :)
Let me know when you get this. I love you.
Your girl,
Lou.

FOUR DAYS LATER: *December*
Lou:
Babe, I'm really worried now. I need to know that you're okay. Please email me back. It's Christmas, and that's the only gift I want from you. To know that you're okay.
I love you.
Lou.

33

LOU

It's Christmas afternoon.

This is normally my favorite holiday, but this year it's a little different. Not because Declan is deployed, but because he hasn't answered any of my emails after telling me he'd be coming home soon.

It's so hard to keep the worry to a minimum, because I don't know what is going on over there and maybe he's just busy. But, the fear of losing him always creeps back in and nearly consumes me. What if something has happened to him?

Then again, wouldn't they have called his mom or notified someone by now?

"Ugh," I mutter to myself.

I haven't left the couch since I arrived an hour ago. My mom's fixing Christmas dinner with Tessa, both of them kicked me out as soon as I stepped inside. Something about my attitude is piss poor and will taint the food.

Now, tell me how that is possible?

The kids are at their little wooden table that sits next

to the dining room table, both of them have an abundance of crayons spread between them while they color different pictures.

Lucy stands, bringing me a picture she's drawn and hands it to me. "What's this?" I ask, smiling at her.

"That you," she points to a dark haired stick figure with what I'm assuming is a dress. "That's me and Lane." She points again. "And our swingset."

"Oh, I love it." I smile. "I like the airplane."

"That's Uncle Declan." She smiles and I fight back the tears. "That's him coming home to us all." She leaves the picture with me and skips back to the table to start another.

She has no idea how she nearly gutted me with such a simple drawing.

God, I hope you're okay. I love you.

I've been staring out the back windows, hoping it snows, at least that would cheer me up a little.

"Have you talked to him today?" Kyle asks, moving around the coffee table and taking a seat beside me.

I shake my head. When Kyle found out I had gone to the airport, he didn't object to it or anything. He was supportive and I think that shocked the shit out of me the most. I just knew that after last time and then him having to tuck his sister into bed for the exact same thing again would send him over the edge and ready to murder Declan, but it didn't.

All he would say is that it was something Declan had to wrap his head around and he feels like he has.

"How you holding up?" He pops a cookie in his mouth.

"Where'd you get that?" I ask, turning my head to look

over the back of the couch at the kitchen where my mom smiles at me. "You gave him a cookie but not me?"

"His attitude doesn't suck." She grabs a cookie of her own and tosses it in her mouth. "Chocolate chip, your favorite."

"Wicked lady." I hide my smile and face back to looking out the window.

"Remember that time we slept down here, convinced we were going to find Santa coming through the chimney?" he asks.

"Yeah, I don't think either of us made it a full hour before we passed out."

"You didn't," our dad says. "I had to come carry you both to your rooms." He heads into the kitchen and plucks a cookie from the platter, causing me to groan in frustration.

Tessa grabs one, brings it over to the couch and holds it out for me. "Now see, this is how family is supposed to treat family."

"Yeah, yeah." My mom waves me off and turns to fixing the macaroni and cheese on the stove.

"How you holding up?" Kyle asks once everyone has returned to their normal job duties.

"I'm just trying to keep my mind from going there." I look over at him, and take a bite of my cookie. "You know?"

"I get it." He rests his arm behind me on the couch and pulls me in closer to him. "He'll be okay, you said he's coming home soon right? Maybe he's just caught up in getting ready for all of that."

"Yeah, maybe." I shrug. One of the kids calls for him and he stands and walks to their little table.

The doorbell rings, but I ignore it. Who could be here on Christmas Day? Granted, nothing surprises me with my parents and it's probably a belated Christmas morning gift. My dad runs his hand along the back of the couch on his way to the door, tugging on a piece of my hair as he passes.

When my eyes focus back on the window, I see it's finally snowing. I stand, walking toward the patio and watch the snowflakes begin to gather against the surface. I open the door, stepping out into the cold air and let the feeling of the snow hit against my face while I try to catch snowflakes on my tongue.

I wish you were here.

"It's beautiful isn't it?"

My heart stops, and I'm terrified to turn around because the person behind me couldn't possibly be real, right? He's not supposed to be home until after Christmas. That's what he told me.

Slowly, I turn around and find Declan stepping through my parent's back door and outside with me. He's dressed in his combat uniform, and I just stare at him. Jaw to the ground, stare at him.

He can't be real. I'm itching to reach out and make sure when he speaks again. "You just going to keep drooling or come and give me a kiss? It's been a long fucking year without one."

"Declan!" I squeal and run toward him. He catches me, wrapping his arms around my ass and lifts me against him. "I've missed you."

"I missed you more, baby. So much more." He spins us both as the snow continues to cascade down on us. "What are you thinking right now?" He sits me on my feet, cups my cheek and stares into my eyes in a way that makes the butterflies in my belly flutter to life.

"That this isn't real."

Declan slowly moves my hand over his chest, resting against his heart. "I can promise you, baby, this is very much real." He leans down, placing a soft kiss to the tip of my nose. "It feels good to be home." He smiles wider than I've seen in a long time. A year to be exact. "For good." He stares at me while his words register, and when they do I suck in a deep breath.

"For good?"

He nods. "For good, baby. My duty is with you now."

Okay, swoon. This man...

"I figured out that I've been wrapped up in my father's death for so long and it is still affecting me after all these years. I couldn't let his death go, I wasn't able to process it. But, it was my dad's duty to serve our country, you were always meant to be mine. I was just too fucking stubborn and fought against myself for too long, and it nearly cost me everything." He runs a hand over my hair, pulling my lips to his.

"You're never leaving me again?"

He shakes his head, my smile growing wider. I love the fact that he's a Marine, it's sexy. Not to mention the body it's built over the years, but I'm more happy that he's going to be home and we can officially start our life together.

"I love you, Lou."

"I love you," I whisper, and we stand there, kissing while the snow falls to our feet and I couldn't imagine a better Christmas surprise.

———

WE FINISH DINNER, and I finally got a cookie without anyone bitching at me for my pathetic attitude. I'm helping my mom clean up the kitchen while Declan plays with my brother and the twins by the tree.

"I'm glad to see that smile back on your face," my mom whispers beside me.

"Me too." I smile, placing the last dish from the sink into the dishwasher. My Christmas started out shitty, filled with worry about Declan and if he was okay, little did I know his silence was part of him surprising me today.

He told me earlier that he'd been told he'd be home on Christmas from the day he learned he would be coming home, he just hid it from me and made me believe it would be after Christmas. And to make matters worse, my own family knew about it. Which is why no one acted strange when the doorbell rang earlier, because they all knew who was on the other side of it.

"So, what are the two of you planning to do now?" Tessa asks, wiping her hands on the rag and tossing it on the counter.

"I'm not sure, but I know that we will finally get to start living again." I sigh in relief as I watch my boyfriend.

Timing is never in our favor, I've learned that. We were apart for fifteen years, and just when we got our second chance at love, he was yanked away for another year.

Some would think that being apart again for so long would be easy, considering that we had just gotten back together when everything happened... but honestly, it fucking sucked.

In the short time that Declan and I decided to put the past behind us and give the two of us a go again, we connected on a level that was deeper than anything we ever had before. I thought I loved that boy, but it's nothing in comparison to the man I love today. We got used to being able to call each other whenever we wanted, him stopping by for a quick lunch date while I was working, or just being able to fall asleep in each other's arms.

"I'm happy he's home." Tessa throws an arm over my shoulder and pulls me into her side.

"Momma," Lane yells from his spot on the floor. "C'mon, I wanna open presents."

"Of course he does." She laughs, dropping her arm and heading toward her spot on the couch next to my brother.

My mom laughs, following behind her to where she starts pulling presents from under the tree. We always spend Christmas evening at my parents, that way Kyle and Tessa get to enjoy their mornings with their kids without feeling rushed to leave by a certain time.

I watch as she starts piling gifts next to everyone, making sure to tell the kids they can't open them yet. Lane is chomping at the bit to rip into the colorful paper and has shook every box my mom sat beside him while Lucy is sitting like the pretty princess she is, patiently waiting. Sometimes it cracks me up that they're even twins whenever they're so different from each other.

I sit next to Declan on the love seat, holding my gifts on my lap while she continues to pass presents out. One of my mom's favorite things is shopping for her kids and grandkids, so they always go above and beyond at Christmas time. She walks back toward where we're sitting and hands Declan a pile of his own gifts, and I can see the shock on his face as she does. He didn't think she'd get him anything, but I knew better than that.

Granted, she knew he was coming home.

His present from me is at my house, nestled underneath the undecorated tree because it just didn't feel right decorating it without having him with me. So I left it.

At least it's prelit... it looks somewhat festive that way. Even if the light on top is hanging by the wire. Oh well. I'll do better next year.

"Alright, everyone dig in," Mom tells us.

Lane squeals and is throwing paper up into the air and behind him as he rips through his presents. The paper he's throwing is landing right on Kyle's lap, which is frustrating him because he is the giant version of his son and is doing the exact same thing, except his paper and the paper Lane has thrown is going behind the couch.

Declan shakes with laughter beside me, watching Lane while he slowly opens his own present on his lap. I look at him just as he freezes, looking into the box on his lap. Leaning toward him, I look over his arm and gasp when I see what's inside.

Declan slowly pulls the ornament from the box and holds it up in front of him, every eye in the room is on us now. My mom stands by the tree, a smile on her face as she glances at my dad.

"Declan, we have a family tradition." She winks at me before turning toward the tree. "Each member of this family adds an ornament to our tree. I have all of my kids' ornaments made in school, I have ones that signify milestones in their lives, I have the grandkids first Christmas, and so many I really can't count them all." She stares at her tree. "But, you didn't have an ornament on our tree, and well, we thought it was time to change that."

Declan shakes his head slowly, his smile growing as he

spins the small combat boots in his hand. "I remember that tradition, I always thought it was cool."

"It's probably my favorite part about the holiday." She winks at him and the two stare at each other for a brief moment. "So, will you come and put your family ornament on our tree?"

Declan slides the presents from his lap and onto the arm of the couch before standing and walking toward the tree. He looks for an empty spot, but let's be honest, with this tree, there aren't many spots to hang much else.

"Just stick it somewhere, Uncle D," Lucy says. "It'll take ya forever if ya don't."

We all laugh, but Declan does as she says and hangs it on a branch near the top before giving my mother a hug and shaking my dad's hand. He drops a kiss to the top of my head before falling back onto the couch beside me.

After we've opened all of our presents, we sit around and watch the kids play with their gifts. Lane got a new train track and has pressed the damn horn a million times, and if it wasn't for the giant smile on his face, I'd have thrown that damn toy outside by now.

Lucy got a new American Girl doll and has changed it's clothes at least eight times and I refuse to brush the doll's hair again.

This Christmas has turned out to be everything I ever could have asked for. It's such a surreal feeling, and one that's so hard to describe. I feel complete, like all the heartache and pain I've gone through was worth it just to have this moment here with my family, with my Declan.

"Looks like there's one more gift under the tree," Mom says, point at a tiny box that is shoved toward the back of the stand. "I must have missed it. Can you grab it, Lou?"

I nod, standing and walking to the tree before dropping to my knees and reaching under the bottom row of branches for the box. When I pull it out, I flip the tag over and realize it's a gift for me from my parents.

"It's for me," I say, turning to look at my mom.

"Aw, man. I was hoping it was one for me." Lane crossed his arms over his chest in annoyance that the last gift wasn't his before Tessa taps him on the shoulder with her foot.

"Well, open it," Lucy shouts, making us all giggle.

"Okay, okay." I swat at her but slowly start pulling at the edges until a small box that looks like Declan's is all I see. When I pull the cardboard lid off, my breath hitches in my throat.

A silver Christmas ornament in the shape of a diamond ring hangs from a white satin ribbon. The writing in the center says *Declan and Lou* with the year below it.

I'm confused, Declan and I aren't engaged so why would they give me an ornament...

Just as the thought hits me, I slowly turn my head to look behind me to see Declan kneeling a few steps away. A red, velvet box is in his hand with a white gold diamond ring sitting in the center of it.

I gasp, feeling the tears start to fall. Is this real? I need to pinch myself to make sure, but I can't because I'm frozen in place by the look in this man's eyes.

"Lou," he clears his throat, "I've been blessed in this life, to have the type of love that we share with each other. It hasn't been easy, and there were times when I never thought we'd make it here." He smiles at me. "I know without a doubt that I'm not good enough for you."

"I'll say," Kyle says jokingly, but it earns him an elbow to the ribs from Tessa.

Declan shakes his head, a smile touching his lips.

"Go on," I urge him, wanting to hear the rest of his proposal so I can give him my answer.

Everyone laughs, and that's when I realize my dad has the camera out and is recording this.

"As I was saying," Declan cuts his eyes to Kyle. "I don't deserve you. I've broken your heart more times than I'd care to admit, and I was selfish for doing it. But, the pull that we have with one another is once in a lifetime. There's only been one girl who holds my heart, and baby, that's you. You take my breath away every time I walk into a room and at the same time, you breathe life back into me. I love you, Lou. And I want to spend the rest of my life with you, no more deployments, no more heartaches, just me and you forever."

I wipe at the tears that I can't control. Forever sounds pretty damn good to me.

"What do you say, beautiful? Will you marry me?" he asks, looking up at me. He almost looks nervous, as if I could ever turn down his proposal.

"Yes!" I scream, sitting the ornament down and standing at the same time he does. I jump into his arms, holding him tightly as he spins us both in a circle and presses his lips to mine.

It's soft, and sweet, and the perfect way to mark this moment.

Once he sits me on my feet, he pulls back and slowly pulls the ring from the box and slides it onto my ring finger.

"It was my mom's ring." He smiles. "I wanted it to be special, and I couldn't think of a better choice for you."

"It's beautiful, Declan." I look down at my hand, enjoying the weight of the small piece of jewelry and the way the diamond catches the light. "It's perfect."

"You're perfect," he whispers, kissing the tip of my nose when I look up at him.

"Come here, baby girl." My dad breaks the moment, pulling me into his arms while my mom does the same to Declan.

Tessa hugs me next, followed by my brother. "I can't believe you're getting married." He smiles at me. "Actually, I can't believe I got married before the two of you."

"Oh, shut up." I hit him in the gut.

"Come here." He laughs, pulling me in for a hug. "I'm happy for you. You deserve this."

"Thanks, Kyle." I pull away, wiping a tear before it has a chance to fall.

"Declan," Kyle says, giving me a chance to regain some composure. "I guess this means we're brother's now."

"I guess so." Declan smiles. "It's about damn time." He looks over at me and winks.

I'll never get tired of that.

EPILOGUE
DECLAN

41 Weeks Later

"You asshole," My wife screams, throwing a pillow at me. "You fucking did this to me."

The day we found out about her pregnancy, we moved the wedding date up. Lou didn't want to give birth without our last names being the same, and I felt the same.

I smile, stepping closer to her hospital bed. "I'm not sorry, baby." I'd lean over to kiss her forehead, but I don't trust that my feisty wife wouldn't take a punch at me right now.

The night I proposed to her, we went back to our house, yes ours because I never left after that night, and I worshiped every inch of her for hours. It wasn't until the next that I realized I hadn't used a condom, and she hadn't been on birth control since I had been overseas. We both talked and decided that we were ready for this, we didn't need anymore time alone and were ready to move on with our lives.

Little did we know, that night was the night we conceived our first child. Fast forward to now and hopefully within the hour I'll be a dad.

"I'm not sorry either," she says right before a contraction barrels through her. She grabs my hand before I can move it.

Yes, move it. Have you ever held a woman's hand during labor? They get this weird freakish strength that can crush a bone with one squeeze. My hands can't take much more of it.

"You're hurting me," I tell her, but she doesn't give a shit.

She squeezes harder and I swear, even though I know she's in pain from the contraction, she smiles a little like she's enjoying this.

"I don't give a fuck," she screams. "You put our son inside me, and I should have known he'd be just as stubborn as your ass. He refused to come out before his due date and he's too big," she cries out.

She's not wrong, we're a week past our due date and were induced today. I'm not sure when he would have decided he was ready if we hadn't.

"Alright, Lou. With this next one, I need you to push down into your bottom while we count it out, okay?"

My wife doesn't respond, instead she just stares at him as if he's forgotten what her profession is.

She looks up at me, and I fall in love with her all over again in that one look. She's so damn beautiful, even laying in a hospital bed with her hair tangled and matted against her sweaty forehead. I don't think she's ever been more beautiful than at this moment, knowing that she's about to give birth to my son.

"I love you," I whisper.

"I lov–" Another contraction hits her. "Hate you."

I chuckle at her change of words, not taking any of it to heart.

"That's good, Lou. That's good," the doctor says. "One more big push."

Lou relaxes at the end of the count and turns her head toward the screen, even during birth she's monitoring herself. I shake my head, she tenses and I know another is coming.

"Ah!" she cries out.

"Last one, Lou," the doctor tells her. "I've got him."

I lean over her knee to see my son enter this world, and I'm blown away at what I see. My wife just did something so amazing, and I don't know how I'll ever be able to repay her.

They take my boy, moving him to another little area in the room where they check his weight and begin wiping him down.

"Is he okay?" Lou tries to sit up. "He's not crying."

Just as she says it, our boy let's out a shrill cry that nearly makes us all cover our ears. Hoorahs and clapping is heard from the other side of the door, and all the grandparents, family, and friends are excited to meet him. Lou relaxes back onto her pillow, when she looks at me my heart shatters.

"I was so worried."

"He's fine, baby. You did good, Momma," I tell her. "I fucking love you so much."

"I love you."

The nurse brings our boy over to us, wrapped in a striped blue hospital blanket and a blue hat covering his head. The dark curls that stick out from underneath the cap tells me he has a head full of hair, meaning the saying is true. If you have heartburn during your pregnancy, your baby will have a head full.

I lean against the side of the bed, my arm draped over the top of Lou's pillow as I watch the nurse place him in Lou's arms. He stops crying almost immediately, sensing who his momma is. She holds him close to her chest, staring down at him with a smile on her face. I reach down, taking his tiny hand in mine and rubbing my thumb over his palm.

"He's perfect," I tell her.

"He is." She smiles up at me, and I cover her lips with mine. When we break apart, she looks down at our boy. "Welcome to the world, Duke Kyle Sanchez."

"Hey, little man."

"Gunnar's going to love him," she tells me.

"I already know it. They'll be the best of friends." I smile, thinking of my dog. He hasn't left our side since I returned home from deployment, and sleeps at the foot of our bed every night. But, I have a feeling that will change now and he'll be sleeping wherever Duke is.

A few minutes later, the door to our room bursts open and all our family and friends pour in. Lou's mom rushes to her side, while my mom all but pushes me out of the way.

"Get used to it. You're not important anymore," Kyle tells me as he rolls his eyes.

"Aw, you're important, baby." Tessa pats his cheek. He smiles at her but it fades when she starts to push away from him. "Let me go meet my nephew."

I have to hold back the laugh.

I stand back, watching everyone fawn over my boy and

drink it all in. I've never been this happy in my life, I have everything I could ever want.

A wife.

A son.

A forever.

The End

THANK YOU

Thank you for taking the time to read One More Night.

Never miss a new release:
https://bit.ly/2N2R27V

Join J. Akridge's ARC team:
https://bit.ly/3gF7uXb

More about J. Akridge's books:
https://www.jakridgeauthor.com

Contact J. Akridge:
Facebook
Instagram
Reader Group
Goodreads
BookBub

ACKNOWLEDGMENTS

To my amazing husband, my biggest supporter.
Without you, I wouldn't be able to write the way I do. You're always offering a listening ear, even when you don't want to hear about the "smut". Thank you for being you and my rock in this life.
To my very best friend, Tori Fox.
I don't even know where to start. I'm so thankful that our paths crossed and we were brought together. You're the very best person and I'm thankful that we'll have many years of friendship to come. You're my biggest cheerleader and always push me to do better! I love you BIG, girl!
The indie community.
Whew. THANK YOU! The support from readers, authors, bloggers, bookstagram mers, TikTokers, etc. You're amazing and I'm so thankful to be part of it.
Of course, thank you to my sweet friend, Nicole and her husband, Steven.
I had a million questions for Declan's character and

they both helped tremendously. Thank you for your service, Steven!

Kari March.

I adore my covers and it's all thanks to you, girl. You're my go to!

To all the bloggers ... I know you're there.

Thank you so much for always supporting me and taking on these new books.

To all of my beta readers.

Thank you for always taking the time to work on my books and find any and everything that can make it that much better for the readers. You do so much for me and I love you all for it.

And finally, thank you to my readers.

Without you, none of this world would be happening. You all keep me motivated more than you know. With every comment, like, share, etc. I see it and I push to give you more. Thank you all for your support and allowing me to continue this dream of writing.

With Love,

ALSO BY J. AKRIDGE

The Hawks Series

Full Court Press

Foul Shot

Bank Shot - 2022

Break Away - 2022

Stand Alone Titles

One Night

One More Night -PreOrder Now

Charged: A Salvation Society Novel

The Tribute Series

Enthralled

Enamoured

Enraptured

ABOUT THE AUTHOR

J. Akridge is a contemporary romance author that has a quirky sense of humor and enjoys sweet, sexy, feel good romance. She likes her bun messy, her sweats comfy, and her coee strong. She resides in Missouri with her husband and their three children, a couple of Great Danes and tiny Yorkie named Jack. She's experiencing her own happily ever after with her high school sweetheart.

Since publishing her first book in 2020, she's been inspired to continue writing the love stories that play out in her head each day.

She loves to hear from her readers so make sure you check her out on social media or sign up for her newsletter to stay up to date on all her latest releases and sales.